Forgotten Memories
A Novel of Mystery, Hope and Triumph

By
Lurma Swinney, PhD

Forgotten Memories

A novel published by SD Publishing House
ISBN: 978-1-63752-291-2
Copyright © 2023 by Lurma Swinney, PhD

All rights reserved. The reproduction, transmission, or utilization of this work in whole or in part in any form by any electronic, mechanical, or other means, now known or hereafter invented, including xerography, photocopy and recording, or in any information storage or retrieval system, is forbidden without written permission. For permission, please contact SD Publishing House Post Office Box 7676 Florence, SC 29502 U.S.A.

This is a work of fiction. Names, characters, places, and incidents are either the product of the author's imagination or are used fictitiously, and any resemblance to actual persons, living or dead, business establishments, events or locales is entirely coincidental.

www.sdpublishinghouse.com
Printed in U.S.A.
Cover designed by Mr. Jay Swinney
Edited by Mrs. Sophia Davis

To my Co-Workers
In the Lee County School District.
Thank you for welcoming me as part of the team.

Acknowledgements:

I give God all the praise and honor that is due to His Holy Name.

Thank you to everyone for supporting me by purchasing my books over the years.

Part One
May

Chapter 1

"Vinny?" a soft, soothing, male's voice called in a distinctive Jamaican accent. "Vinny, can you hear me? Wake up, honey." The comatose woman opened her drowsy, brown eyes slowly and focused on the small television mounted in the corner of the wall; the white, porcelain sink adorned with a plastic water bottle and a food tray; a slew of beautiful flowers, plants, balloons and cards; a red-headed, freckled-face Caucasian male doctor in blue scrubs staring at her; a Caucasian nurse in flowery-printed scrubs to the side of the doctor, and a dark-chocolate-tanned, Jamaican man, positioned in front of the hospital bed where she lay, smiling at her with perfect, pearly-white teeth. She cringed as an overwhelming sense of fright enveloped her pecan-tanned face. "Hi, sleepyhead," the dark-chocolate-tanned man continued with a smile glued to his strong, chiseled features.

"Mrs. Perkins, I'm Dr. Malone. How do you feel?" the tall, slinky, Caucasian doctor probed.

"Where... what happened?" the weakened woman squeezed out of dry, chapped lips.

"You were in an accident," the doctor confirmed. "Do you remember the accident?" She shook her head slowly. "Well, that's okay. Let me check your vitals. You've been in a coma for six weeks. Welcome back." His smile was friendly.

Catching her hand, the Jamaican man added, still exposing all thirty-twos, "It's so good to see you finally awake, Vinny." His five-foot-eleven-inch frame was muscular. He wasn't what you might call drop-dead gorgeous, but he was attractive with the clean-shaven face and extremely low, almost bald haircut, with a distinct, small mole characterizing his left cheek.

"Vinny...?" she repeated with a slight frown, trying desperately to understand what was unfolding in her surroundings. "My name is Vinny?" The Jamaican man slowly focused on the doctor in a dazed glare.

"Don't worry, Mr. Perkins. It's not uncommon for a victim of an accident as severe as your wife's to have a little temporary memory loss," Dr. Malone explained then focused back on his patient. "Mrs. Perkins, what is the last thing you remember?"

The confused woman rubbed across her medium-length, kinky black hair then focused her light brown eyes on the doctor and stammered, "I...I don't remember anything. I don't even remember my name." She paused, stretching her eyes wide then added, "I don't know who *any* of you are." She paused again with tears forming in her frightened, fluttering eyes. "My God! I don't remember...*anything*?"

Chapter 2

"Parker!"

"Yes!"

"Where are you?"

"Right here," the six feet tall, boyishly handsome, biracial man answered, entering from a back room of an art studio, which displayed paintings on the paneled walls. He was cleaning a paint brush, wearing a baseball cap turned backward over his short, curly black hair. "Oh, hi Shelby."

"Hi. Have you seen Valencia today?" the tall, skinny, Caucasian lady in a stylish, fuchsia, two-inches-above-the-knee, rayon skirt suit and gray pumps asked, pushing her dyed-blonde bangs out of her thin face, with the rest of her bouncy blonde hair in a short stylish bob with the left side pushed behind her ear. She stood right at five-eleven in her three-inch heels and stood almost eye-to-eye with the young man.

"No, not yet. She is scheduled to go home today," he shared, preoccupied with his task. "Come in the back. I need to finish cleaning these brushes."

Following him into the back room with clacking heels, Shelby wanted to know, "Does she have her memory back yet? Her show is in two months."

"Not yet."

"What're we going to do?!" she shrieked.

He chuckled, "It'll be fine, Shelby. She already has almost all of her pieces ready for the show."

"What a thing to happen!" she raged, lighting a cigarette. "Right around the corner from her big show!"

"We'll be ready."

"*We*?!" she yelped. "What'd you mean...*we*?!"

"Vinny is letting me display some of my pieces in the show," he proudly announced.

"*What*?! She never told me that!"

"She doesn't have to tell you *everything*, Shelby. You're just her *manager*," he chuckled, dripping with sarcasm.

"She most *certainly* does!" she insisted. "I arranged this show, and the buyers are expecting *Valencia Perkins'* work."

"And they *will* get Valencia Perkins' work, with a *bonus* of Parker Grayson's!"

"Humph!" she grunted. "You are her *assistant*, Parker. Don't get it confused."

"I won't if you won't," he singsong.

"You said she's going home today?" she finalized, heading for the door.

"Um hum," he mumbled, thinking that Shelby would make *coffee* nervous, with all her energy.

****

Valencia Perkins hesitantly strolled her five-feet-four-inches tall frame into the thirty-five-hundred-square-feet, two-story, brick house in a pair of black denim jeans, a turquoise, button-down, cotton blouse, and black sneakers. Her concerned husband trailed closely behind her, watching her every response to the life that was buried somewhere in her distant memory. "I don't remember *any* of this," she finally admitted.

He placed the many flowers, plants, balloons, cards, and small overnight bag on both the table and the floor and moved slowly to his wife. "Vinny, the doctor said it's going to take time for you to regain your memory. You suffered a terrible blow to the head in that accident."

"What kind of accident was it?"

"Car accident."

"Was anyone else involved or did I hit a tree or something?"

"You went over an embankment."

"Ouch!" she chuckled, and he shared her smile. She turned and focused on her husband, standing there in those neatly pressed blue jeans, maize polo shirt, and navy-blue sneakers and wondered what kind of life they shared. "How long have we been married?"

"Three *wonderful* years."

She picked up a picture from the coffee table and observed the big smiles she and her husband shared, and she felt delighted at how happy they appeared. "What is my name again?"

"Valencia McDonald Perkins, but everyone calls you Vinny, except Shelby, your manager."

"I…I'm sorry," she stuttered, feeling a little embarrassed to ask. "And *your* name?"

"Don't be sorry," he coaxed with a shaky voice, feeling a little sad that she had to ask at all. "Chazmond Perkins, but everyone calls me Chaz." It was heart-wrenching for him to witness his wife in so much pain, desperately trying to remember her life. "Would you like to soak in a nice, hot bath to relaxed, honey?" She thought for a moment, just staring at him. "I'll order Chinese, and while we're eating, I will answer all your questions."

Nodding slowly, she responded, "That sounds great."

****

"Hi, sweetie," spoke a stocky, average-height, light-brown man with graying beard and mustache in construction worker's clothes. He was carrying a lunch box and a brick mason's lever as he planted a kiss on his wife's cheek, while she stood at the stove, stirring the contents in a steaming pot.

"Hi. How was your day?" she greeted him back, taking his lunch box, and placing it in the sink.

"It was okay," he answered, patting her round behind. "How was yours?"

Smiling, she responded, "It was busy. I think we had over eight hundred hungry diners today."

"Really?"

"Yes, and I'm exhausted," she explained, running water into the sink. She was a short lady, only five feet one inch with a protruding behind and stomach, but not grossly overweight. Her short hair was slicked back on her head, exposing her round pecan-tanned face, slight double-chin, and slight overbite. Her brown eyes were covered with plastic-framed, brown, oval-shaped eyeglasses.

"Patrice, how is Vinny?" he asked, standing in the doorframe.

"She still can't remember anything, but she went home today."

"Oh, that's good," he acknowledged as a tall, slim, dark-skinned young man entered the kitchen with his blue jeans sagging off his hips, oversized white T-shirt, uncombed, kinky hair, and earrings in his earlobes, as well as fire-breathing dragon tattoos all over his exposed arms and neck.

"Ma, you ain't finished cooking yet?" the young man snarled, searching the refrigerator for something to eat.

"*You* could've cooked, Frankie," his mother snapped. "I *worked* all day."

"And what about you, young man," his father added. "Did *you* find a job today?"

"Nobody's hiring, Dad," the young man defended.

"Yeah right!" his father sarcastically countered. "You need to look harder." Frankie snarled as his father took a deep breath. "I'm gonna take a shower."

"Okay, honey. Dinner will be ready by the time you finish," his wife announced as he left.

"How's Vinny?" Frankie asked, changing the subject, and dropping in a chair at the table.

"She went home today," his mother answered.

"Her memory back?"

"Not yet."

"I ain't never heard of no *black* person having *amnesia*."

"Well, you have *now*…your *sister*!" his mother sarcastically retorted.

****

"Did you have a nice bath, honey?" Chaz asked Vinny as she joined him in the den on the couch in front of the television set. She was wearing white, soft-cotton pajamas, while he still wore his jeans.

"Yes, I did. Thank you," she responded. He pulled a small, folding table in front of her and placed a plate of Chinese food on it. "They deliver?"

"Um hum," he confirmed, as he placed his food on another folding tray then sat on the couch beside her.

After taking a bite, she acknowledged, "It's good."

"Yes, it's our favorite," he made known then took a breath. "Okay *ask*."

"What?"

"Ask your questions. Anything you want to know."

"I noticed some paintings in the hallway with my name on them. Do I paint?"

"Yes, you do. That's your profession. You are an artist," he explained.

"Awesome."

"You have a show coming up. Shelby is going ballistic, wondering if you'll be ready."

"I bet so," she chuckled. "Where do I work?"

"Sometimes, you paint in the basement. But you do much of your work at your studio."

"I have a *studio*?!"

"Yes. I gave it to you for a wedding present."

"Wow! That's very generous. Where is it?"

"Downtown, in the heart of the city. You do very well, too," he explained. "Your assistant is Parker. You probably don't remember him, but he visited you in the hospital."

"So many people were coming in and out. I can't say that I do."

"It's okay. The doctor said that going back into the studio and painting might help you to remember."

"I'd like that. If for no other reason, to see if I remember *how* to paint," she laughed.

"The doctor said people with amnesia usually remember their craft," he shared, smiling with her.

"What about you. What do you do?"

"I'm a principal at a hybrid high school."

"What's hybrid?"

"That means we have both eLearning and face-to-face learning."

"Wow! That's different but nice."

"A little challenging sometimes, but I like it. We're piloting the program this year, so we're still working out the kinks."

"Are the students and parents adjusting to it well?"

"Yes. They have a choice to attend either face-to-face or virtual."

"Why did they decide to pilot this program?"

"Because many of our students work to help their families, we felt that we needed to be flexible with their education," he explained.

"How are the teachers teaching virtually?"

"There are several eLearning platforms that we're using. Teachers can actually have face-to-face instruction with students online."

"Cool."

"Yes, it is."

"What?" she wheedled, noticing his beaming glow as she smiled with him.

"That's what you said when this first started, that it was *cool* to teach students online," he clarified.

"So, I haven't forgotten *everything*," she reacted.

He came back with, "Maybe not, sweetheart."

"How long did we know each other before we got married?"

"We were high school sweethearts. I moved here from New York when we were both seniors. My dad's job transferred him. I fell in love with you at first sight, and you said you liked my accent."

She chuckled, "Really?"

"Yeah, but I think you liked these muscles," he laughed, flexing his arms. "I was on the wrestling team, and you used to come to *every* match."

"Really?"

"So, I *had* to win with you sitting there!" he announced jovially.

"That's interesting."

Sobering, he reminisced with a smile, "But we drifted apart a little when I went to college, and you went to art school. But, as soon as I saw you again, I knew I had to have you."

"How long did you have to go to school to be a principal?"

"Well, I had to teach for a few years. Then I went back and earned my master's in administration and then my doctorate."

"You have a *doctorate*?!" she exploded.

He smiled proudly as he answered back, "Yes. A Ph.D."

"I'm impressed. Do I have a degree?"

"Yes, you have a B.A. in art."

"That's *it*?" she laughed, and he joined her. "I'm married to a *doctor*, and I only have a *bachelors*?!"

"Yes, but *you* make more money," he shared her laughter then sobered gradually. "It's so nice to hear you laugh, Vinny."

"It feels good to laugh," she agreed then took a bite of food. "What month is it?"

"May."

She yawned and announced, "I shouldn't be after sleeping for six weeks, but I'm tired."

"You had a full day," he recognized, getting up and taking the food from her table. "Go to bed, honey. I'll be up soon. I'll clean up, take a shower, and then check on you." She nodded, and he planted a kiss on her forehead.

She couldn't help but to think how perfect this man seemed. Is it possible to be so happy and not remember? Or was her brain trying to hide something terrible from her so she *wouldn't* remember? She still had a lot of questions, but she was just too tired to absorb any more information tonight. The doctor said that all the swelling in her brain had gone down, so her memory loss wasn't physical. What happened to her to cause her to blot out her life? *She felt so frightened. Why?*

****

"Vinny Perkins came out of her coma," a person wearing a pinky ring with a snake engraved around it announced on the telephone.

"I know," the person on the other end of the telephone replied. "But she has amnesia."

"Yes, that's true."

"What is Frankie saying?"

"Not much. She's his sister. We can't expect him to be totally onboard."

"What do we do if she starts to remember?"

"We do what we do with any other loose end," the person replied sternly. "We tie it up...*permanently*!"

****

"Patrice, you know Frankie needs to get a job!"

"I know he does, Milo, but I'm trying to be patient with him," she agreed, getting into bed with her husband in a huge, pink nightshirt.

"He has nothing but excuses."

"I know," she understood. "Can't you get him a job on the construction crew with you?"

"And have him *embarrass* me?!" he exploded in laughter, and she chuckled with him. "Get him a job with you at the restaurant!"

"And have him embarrass *me*?!" she mocked him in laughter.

He sobered. "His sisters are doing so well. I don't know what happened to that boy."

"I don't know either. Vinny has her own art studio, and Justine is in college to be a nurse. Where did we go wrong with Frankie?"

"The hell if I know!" They burst into laughter together.

****

"Are you all right, honey?" Chaz asked, sliding into bed with his wife in his boxer shorts only. Vinny nodded, but she couldn't help but admire her husband's gorgeous, hairy chest and six pack. She couldn't remember, and although he was joking, she felt that she probably did attend those wrestling matches to check out his beautiful, dark, lean body.

"Where are you from, Jamaica?"

"Yes, I am," he revealed. "I thought my accent was gone."

"Not completely," she shared, as he pulled her in his strong, muscular arms.

"Are your parents in Jamaica?"

"No. When my father retired, they moved back to New York. My mother is Jamaican, but my father is American," he shared.

"Do you have siblings?"

"Yes. I have two brothers, both married with children, but no sisters though. Trevor is the oldest. He's an architect. He and his family live in California. He's married to Melody, who is Puerto Rican, and they have one very smart twelve-year-old little girl name Jennifer," he explained. "Dontae is in the middle. He owns three furniture stores. He lives in New Jersey. His wife is Leslie, who owns a daycare. They have a set of eight-year-old twins, one boy, Josh, and one girl, Natalie. I have one loveable aunt named Nancy, who is my dad's sister. She lives in New York also. Like your mother, Aunt Nancy *loves* to cook. My mother's family is in Jamaica." He took a breath. "That's enough about me for now. I don't want to overload you." He laughed.

She chuckled with him and admired, "You have a beautiful laugh."

"Thank you," he accepted, then added very softly, "I love you, Vinny." Then he planted a soft kiss on her forehead.

She just stared at him momentarily then added softly, "This is so miserable. I wish I could remember!"

He squeezed her closer and expressed, "You will, baby. You will." He took a deep breath. "I thought I was going to lose you. I thank God for sparing your life. Your memory will come back in time." He kissed her forehead again and pulled her closer. Chaz wanted to make love to his wife so badly, but he didn't want to rush her.

Vinny wondered if her husband wanted to make love to her. She was glad he didn't try because she really wasn't in the mood to be intimate with him. She didn't know him. He was a stranger to her. Although it felt good and safe to be in his arms, that's all she wanted right now. She hoped he understood.

Chapter 3

"Hi Chaz! Where's my girl?!" squealed a perky, blonde-headed, light-brown, African American woman, rushing pass Chaz and into the house. Her weaved blonde hair was straight and hung to the middle of her back with neat bangs in the front, down to her neatly trimmed, arched eyebrows. She was shapely built in her skin-tight, gold tights and off-the-shoulder, short, burgundy blouse, exposing a bright red, rose tattoo on her right shoulder. Her make-up was flawless, and her jewelry was excessive. She was of medium height, at five feet, five inches, one hundred and twenty, shapely pounds with six-inch heels that lifted her to the height of Chaz.

"Diamond, what're you doing here so early?" requested Chaz, standing in neat khaki pants and a short-sleeved, navy polo shirt.

"I wanna see my girl! Where is she?!" she squeaked in her high-pitched, southern drawl, as Vinny entered in a knee-length blue jumper and sandals, exposing her thick, smooth brown legs. "*Vinny*!!!" Diamond screamed when she spotted her friend. She jumped to Vinny, grabbed her, and hugged her tightly. Although Vinny smiled, she had no idea who this exotic-looking, gorgeous woman was. "You look great! You lost some weight, girlfriend!"

"We must be friends," Vinny assumed when the woman finally released her.

"Since *junior* high!" she excitedly shrieked. "I just came by to see you. I know you have a million things to do. I'll see you after work." Vinny nodded slowly. Diamond planted a kiss on Vinny's cheek then whirl-winded out the door just as quickly as she had blown through it.

Vinny focused on her husband, smiled wide and asked, "Who in the heck was that?!"

"Diamond Walters, your *best* friend," he chuckled.

"She's exhausting!"

He laughed and replied, "Wait 'til you meet Shelby!"

"And who is Shelby again?"

"Your manager."

"Are we friends too?"

"I guess you could say that. She's helped to make you a lot of money."

She giggled, "I like her already." Vinny's natural, kinky hair was encircled by a blue band, and her one-hundred seventy pounds made her appear a little pudgy at only five feet, four inches, but she wore it well, having no protruding stomach. Her weight settled on her butt and thighs, which is what attracted Chaz to her in the first place.

"Are you okay, baby?" he asked, moving to her, and she nodded. "You do look great."

"She said I lost weight. I must've been a pig before," she joked.

"No!" he chuckled with her. "You were always beautiful to me." He planted a sweet kiss on her forehead.

"You seem too good to be true, Mister!" she teased.

"So are you, Mrs. Perkins," he jested back then sobered quickly. "Are you going to work today?"

"Yes. The doctor said I need to get back into my routine, and besides, I have a show coming up, right?"

Nodding, he confirmed, "Yes, you do." Then he offered, "I'll drop you off."

"I don't drive?"

"Of course, you do, but I thought…"

"I'll drive," she cut him off. "I've got to live my life. I do have a car, don't I?"

"Your BMW was totaled in the accident, but we have a little spare Toyota Corolla," he explained. "You probably don't know how to get to your studio, but I'll write the address down for you to enter into your GPS."

****

"Is she getting her memory back yet?" the person wearing the snake-decorated, pinky ring asked on the cell phone.

"No. I don't think she will get it back?" Frankie hypothesized on his cell phone, sitting in a booth in the back of a dimly lit bar, puffing on a cigarette.

"Why don't we just take care of her now before it's too late?"

"Because she's my *sister*, and besides, I don't want to risk it," Frankie rejected, receiving a beer from the barmaid.

"Listen, I don't want that bitch to finger us!"

"She won't!" he insisted. "I tell you; she can't remember shit!"

"If she starts remembering, you know what we have to do!"

Frankie took a deep breath then confirmed, "Yes…I know!"

****

Vinny was impressed as she pulled in front of a classy, red brick studio with *Valencia Perkins Originals* dangling on the brightly, decorated sign. The building was decorated with a depiction of African culture at the entrance. The glass double-doors and two bay windows were outlined by small paintings of the same with a gold border encircling them. Vinny couldn't believe the immaculate taste she possessed. The studio was gorgeous and surrounded by nice retail stores that reeked of money. Her husband must've paid a small future for it.

She exited the car and slowly strolled to the door, absorbing every viewpoint in the area. When she entered the door, Parker quickly approached her, smiling wide. "Hiya, Boss," he extended greetings, taking her bag and jacket.

"Hi....ah..."

"*Parker*," he finished. "How do you feel?" He handed her a black smock and walked behind a counter to secure her belongings.

"Confused," she admitted, instinctively slipping the smock on over her clothes. She assumed he was her assistant that her husband told her about because he seemed very efficient.

"I bet you are," he understood. "Get paint all over your hands, and you should feel right at home." She smiled with him as the door flew open and Shelby stormed in.

"Valencia, it's great to see you!" she exploded, grabbing Vinny in her arms, and squeezing her tight. "We missed you, girl!" Vinny checked out the obviously stylish woman, in her short, body-fitting green dress, tanned high heels with immaculate jewelry, make-up and hair, to see if she could spark an ounce of recognition. "Parker tells me that you're featuring some of his work in your show. Is this true?"

"Shelby, what part of *amnesia* don't you understand?" he sarcastically probed.

Vinny's dazed eyes darted back and forth from her young assistant to her manager, standing there, staring at her, then she stammered softly, "I...I'm sorry, I...I don't remember anything."

"Pity!" Shelby remarked. "Listen, Valencia, this show is for *you*. Parker can have his own show later. I'll help him."

"Don't talk about me like I'm not here, Shelby," he snapped.

"I'm sorry, Parker, but this is *Valencia's* show!" she held her ground. "Don't you understand that?"

"Shelby, if I promised Parker that he could display his work at the show, I can't very well go back on my word, can I?" Vinny reasoned.

"But you should've checked with me before you made such a drastic decision, Valencia."

"I'm sorry," Vinny repeated. "It'll be great. You're see." At least, she hoped it would be. She had no idea what either Parker or she had painted.

Shelby blew hard then turned to leave, but did an about-face and demanded, "Your work better be splendid, Parker! My reputation is on the line!" Then she stormed out with those clicking heels. Parker and Vinny caught each other's gaze then burst into laughter.

****

"Chaz, three parents called you. Their children need Chromebook replacements," announced a short, milk-chocolate-tanned lady, handing him some notes, as he was entering his spacious office. She was flamboyantly dressed in a tightly fitted, mid-thigh-length, gray skirt with a sleeveless, pink blouse tucked in at the waist, six-inch, dark gray pumps, caked-on makeup, and curly, auburn weaved hair, hanging just below her shoulders.

"Okay, Monica. I'll call them back. Did they say when they could come to pick up the Chromebooks?"

"No. I didn't ask them. I know Chase is at that conference. Will he be back to issue Chromebooks?"

"He left some on the counter in the Media Center for us to issue."

"Okay. I could call the parents back if you want."

"I'll do it. Thank you."

"How is Vinny?"

"She's trying desperately to cope."

"Still can't remember, huh?" she queried, and he shook his head. "I'm sorry. That must be hard on both of you."

"It is. The hardest thing is the way she looks at me. Like I'm a stranger, and she doesn't know what to expect from me," he explained as his telephone began to ring. "Thanks. Monica." She nodded as she left, almost bumping into an older white man with thinning, grayish-brown hair, horn-rimmed eyeglasses, and a winning smile.

"Hi, Monica," he greeted, enjoying the view of her large breasts in the low-cut blouse.

"Hi, Bobby," she replied. "How are you?"

"Great *now*," he flirted.

"Uh huh!" she grunted, walking off, knowing that he was looking at her butt as she walked away, and she smiled.

Bobby McNeil was one of the assistant principals. He had been at the school for over twenty years and was offered the principal's position before they hired Chaz, but he turned it down. He was fifty-six at the time and didn't want to take on that much responsibility at his age. Bobby was incredibly happy to have Chaz, who he admitted was the best principal he had ever worked for these six years. "Come on in here, old man, and quit drooling over my secretary," Chaz laughed, and Bobby joined in the laugher with him.

"She's nice to look at, but I think that little filly has her sights set on *you*, brother." He continued to laugh.

"*Me*?!" Chaz exploded. "Are you nuts?! I am a married man!"

Bobby shot him a quizzical stare and added, "I don't think she cares."

****

"Here you go, Vinny," Parker offered, handing her a cup of coffee in her favorite, butterfly-decorated mug.

"Oh, thank you," Vinny accepted, putting her brush down and receiving the mug.

"That's coming along great," he admired the painting she was working on, as he sipped on his coffee.

She took a deep breath then shared, "You know, Parker, this is the only thing I've done since my accident that feels comfortable."

"You're a pro. This is your life. It *should* feel comfortable," he agreed as they sat on opposite benches.

"So, what's your story, pretty boy?" she inquired, and he chuckled.

"What'd you mean?"

"How did you become my assistant?"

He took a deep breath, smiled, and shared, "Well, as a matter of fact, I want to be an artist too. I went to one of your shows, and I was deeply impressed. I asked you if you needed help, and you said to come by and talk to you, and the rest is history."

"Are you in school?"

"I finished art school a couple years ago, but I've learned more from you than I learned in four years of art school."

"Wow! Thank you," she beamed.

"It's true. You are so talented," he admired. "And generous to a fault. When you asked if I wanted to display some of my pieces at your show, I knew I had made the right decision to come and work for you."

"How long have you been my assistant?"

"Almost two years now."

"Do you like it?"

"*Love* it," he concurred.

"So, how many girlfriends do you have?"

"Just one," he continued, smiling sheepishly.

"Only *one*?" she responded. "A good-looking young man like you?"

He chuckled, "And she would *kill* me if she even *thought* I was looking at anyone else?"

Sharing his laughter, Vinny asked, "What does she do?"

"She's a dancer."

"Wow. I bet she's beautiful."

"Yes, she is."

"Marriage in your future?"

"I suppose so. Some day. When I'm rich and famous like you," he laughed.

"That's nice, Parker," she laughed with him. "But I don't think I'm rich!"

"You don't have to have money to be rich, Vinny, and I think a person with your talent is *very* rich!"

"Touché!" Vinny agreed, holding up her mug in an air toast and he followed her gesture.

"But *you're* also rich in *money*, Mrs. Perkins," he added.

"Are you *serious*?!" she chuckled.

"Vinny, I have seen several of your paintings sell for over ten thousand dollars," he stressed. "I'm not a mathematician, but I would say that you are *pretty* comfortable."

"Wow!" she replied then stopped suddenly, closing her eyes, and shaking her head.

"What's wrong?" he asked, springing up and rushing to her.

"Whew, I just had a flash of something."

"What was it? Do you think it was a memory?"

"I don't know," she answered, putting her coffee on the bench where she sat. "I think I saw someone ...*murdered*."

****

"That's great!" Diamond enthusiastically replied, sitting at her desk in her office at work. "We will have your contract drawn up, and we can meet tomorrow to finalize our business." She paused as a large, elderly, Caucasian man entered in a tailor-made, dark blue suit. She waved him in as she finished her call, and he sat in front of her desk. "Okay, we'll see you tomorrow. I look forward to working with you." Diamond hung up the phone and screamed. "We have Toledo Toys!" He smiled with her.

"That's great, Diamond," he said, sharing her enthusiasm. "That's a really big catch. Congratulations!"

Putting on her heels under her desk, Diamond asked, "What can I do for you, Mr. Kline?" Mr. Kline was the founder and CEO of the advertising company where Diamond worked. He built the company over thirty years ago, and now has seven partners in the firm.

"I just need to talk to you about something."

"Is anything wrong?"

"Oh, no. I have been reviewing your work."

Diamond was growing impatient. She knew she brought in more clients than anyone else in the firm, and the only reason she hadn't made partner yet was because she was black and a woman. There was only one female partner and one black partner, and that was probably their quota. She didn't stand a chance. She reluctantly inquired, "And?"

"And I think it's time we made you a *partner*," he stated and watched Diamond's mouth fly open. "Well, do you accept?"

"A *partner*? *Me*?" She finally found her voice.

"Yes," he confirmed, standing. "It's long overdue. Your appointment has already been approved by the partners." He paused. "Well, I have never seen *Diamond Walters* speechless." He burst into laughter, and Diamond sobered.

"Thank you, Mr. Kline. I really appreciate this."

Heading for the door, he added, "You deserve it. We will announce your partnership at the annual banquet."

She jumped to him, hugging him tight as she yelped, "Thank you! Thank you! Thank you!"

****

"Hey, you're home?!" Chaz acknowledged when he walked into the kitchen and spotted Vinny standing over the stove.

"Yeah, I got a lot done today, so I left early."

"Anything wrong?"

Turning to face him, she announced, "I had a memory flash today," she shared. "At least, I *think* it was a memory."

"That's great, honey!"

"Not so great. I think I witnessed a murder."

"A *murder*?!" he shrieked, and she nodded. "Do you know who the victim was?"

"No. It was so quick."

Pulling her in his arms, he cooed, "Oh, baby, you must've been so scared."

"It was a little frightening."

"Do you think we need to call the police?"

"And tell them what? That I saw a body falling, but I couldn't see the person's face or the person who shot him? They'll think I'm crazy."

"I see what you mean," he agreed. "What do you want to do?"

"Do you remember the doctor suggested that it might be helpful for me to see a therapist?" she asked, and he nodded. "That might be a good idea."

"I agree," he concurred. "Maybe a therapist would be able to help you remember quicker."

"That's what I'm hoping," she held. "Any suggestions?"

"No, but we could ask the doctor."

She nodded. "I'll call him tomorrow."

"Um, something smells good. What is it, spaghetti?" he questioned.

"Yes."

"Um, I love spaghetti."

"Good."

"How was work today?"

"Productive. I think I still remember how to paint. At least, that's what Parker said," she shared.

He smiled with her. "I'm sure he's right." He turned to leave. "I'm going to take a shower." Although Vinny nodded, her mind was still on the person who was murdered. If she was in a place to witness a person being murdered, what does that say about *her*?

****

Diamond sauntered into her luxurious condo still beaming from her news about her partnership when suddenly, she froze, witnessing a six-foot-five-inch, dark-chocolate man seated on her couch looking at television, wrapped in a towel, exposing huge tattoos on his back and chest. He had dreams of being drafted by the NBA, but a busted knee shattered that dream, so he now coached basketball at the local college. "Jake, what in the hell are you doing here?!" she spat.

"Hi, baby," he greeted, standing, and strolling slowly to her.

"What're you doing here?!"

"Just watching Mayor Carson talking about cleaning up crime," he answered, indicating a distinguished-looking, almond-tanned man on the television set.

"I mean, how did you get in my home?!" she demanded.

He hunched his shoulders and nonchalantly stated, "My key."

"I thought you gave all my keys back to me when I asked you for them!"

"I made a copy," he smirked, exposing slightly crooked teeth.

"*What*?!"

She held out her hand, kicked off her heels, and demanded, "Give me my keys, Jake!"

"Come on, baby, don't be like that."

"You broke up with me. Remember? You wanted *Angela*, so you can have her!"

"I made a mistake."

"Tough!" she countered sarcastically.

"Can't you forgive me, baby?" he begged, kissing her neck.

"No. You hurt me!"

"I'm sorry, baby, but I'm here now."

Pushing him back, she came back with, "Yeah, but for how long? Until someone else comes along that tickles your fancy?!"

"No, baby, I learned my lesson," he promised, finding her lips, and kissing her hard. "I'm here to stay."

"No, Jake. I want you to leave!" she stressed, pushing him away again. "I know you don't expect me to just jump into bed with you after you walked out on me for another woman!" She took a breath and raised a quizzical eyebrow. "What happened? Did she dump you like *you* dumped *me*?"

"No! *I* ended it. I realized that I want you and *only* you," he vowed, dropping his towel, exposing his entire body to her, and she swallowed hard. She really did miss him. He was the best lover she ever had. "Come on, baby. You know you want me." He kissed her long and passionately.

"I hate you," she squeezed in between kisses.

"You love me," he cooed, picking her up, wrapping her legs around his nude body.

"I hate you," she weakened as they kissed hard.

"You wished you did," he uttered between kisses.

Chapter 4

"Would you like something to drink, Vinny?"

"No. I'm good," she rejected, taking a seat. "Do I lie down?"

"Not unless you want to," the therapist responded cheerfully and taking the seat opposite Vinny.

"I've never been to a shrink before."

"It's okay. It's like talking to a good friend, with *one* difference."

"What's that?"

"You never have to worry about this friend betraying you and telling *anyone*," the average height, Caucasian lady made known.

Dr. Chloe Bruce is a five-foot-six-inch, forty-five-year-old psychologist. She is plain-looking with little make-up on her face and a plain, two-piece, brown, business suit. She wore her mousy-brown hair in a bun resting in the back of her head. She wasn't ugly but she wasn't pretty either; only plain with no flair at all. "Do you remember anything before the accident, Vinny?"

"No, but I did have a flashback once."

"What was it?"

"I think I saw a murder."

"A *murder*?"

"Yes, but I didn't see the victim *or* the murderer."

"Vinny, until you can remember everything, I wouldn't tell too many people about this," she advised, and Vinny's eyes ballooned. "You see, if you witnessed a murder, and the murderer thinks you can identify him…" She took a breath. "…you might be in *danger*."

****

"Hi, Ma!"

"Frankie, what're you doing here?" his mother squealed, glaring at her son from behind the counter in the busy restaurant.

"Can I get a couple bucks?"

"No," she answered firmly.

"Ma, I'll pay you back?"

"How? You don't have a job," she countered, walking from behind the counter.

"I will," he insisted, as she took his elbow and lead him to the door.

"Frankie, I will *not* give you any money. Now please leave. I'm working."

"Just ten dollars, Ma!"

"No. Not a *dime*!"

****

"Gee! I never thought about being in danger," Vinny finally replied.

"I don't want to scare you, but I do want to caution you," Dr. Bruce expounded, and Vinny nodded.

"I understand."

Changing the subject, the doctor asked, "What kind of relationship do you have with your husband now?"

Smiling, Vinny announced, "Chaz is so nice, it's unbelievable."

"Have you resumed your intimacy with him?"

"No."

"Why not?"

"I don't know," she pondered. "I guess because he's a stranger, and I don't feel comfortable having *sex* with a *stranger*."

Dr. Bruce smiled. "Vinny, you do realize that he *isn't* a stranger, don't you? He's your *husband*."

"I know but it's how I feel."

"Do you have feelings for him? I mean, do you sleep together?"

"Yes, we do, and he hugs me in bed," she explained. "It seems so natural to him."

"It *is* natural to him, Vinny. You're his *wife*, and he loves you," the doctor enlightened the confused woman. "Don't you get urges to be intimate with your husband?"

"Of course. He's a *hunk*," she chuckled.

"Then go with your feelings. The more you embrace your life, the quicker you might get your memory back," the doctor clarified. "I mean, you wouldn't want him to find romance someplace else, would you?"

****

"Chaz, here is the list of teachers who aren't putting in grades like they should," Monica revealed, entering his office with another short skirt on her shapely body.

"How many is it?" he questioned, not even looking up.

"Only four," she revealed. "But parents are complaining."

"One time we had trouble with over half the teachers not putting in grades in a timely manner, so that's an improvement."

"Yes, it is."

"Did you notify Brooke?" he inquired, focusing on her for the first time.

"No."

"Why not? She's the AP for curriculum and instruction."

"I don't know. I didn't think about it. When people call, they ask for *you*."

"I understand that, but Brooke can't do her job if she doesn't know," he explained. "Please share this with her."

"Sure. No problem," she concurred.

"Thanks, Monica," he acknowledged.

"Is Vinny doing any better?"

"Yeah, she's coming around. Hopefully, she'll start remembering soon."

"Great," she verbalized, leaning over his desk, so he could get a good look at her cleavage, but he didn't seem impressed when he did notice her.

"If you need to talk, you know where to find me," she whispered then sauntered out, switching her curvaceous hips.

****

Vinny strolled into her studio and dropped her purse in a cabinet. "Parker!" she called.

"Hi," he answered, coming from the back with a paint brush in his hand.

"Hi. Are you painting?"

"Yeah. Wanna see?"

"Sure," she consented, following him into the back room, pulling on her smock.

"Here it is," he stated, pointing to the painting that he was working on before she arrived.

"Looking good, Parker."

"Really?" he beamed. Her approval meant a lot to him.

"Yeah. You're getting there, kiddo!"

He grabbed her and hugged her tightly. "Thank you, Vinny."

"You're welcome," she grinned as they heard the front door open. "I'll get it. You keep working."

"Hello," she said to the visitor.

"Hi, big sis," Frankie responded, and she raised an eyebrow. "Oh, I forgot. You have *amnesia*!" he joked. "How does it feel? That shit can't be any fun."

"No, it isn't," she established. "I'm sorry, I don't remember your name."

"Frankie," he articulated.

"And you're my *brother*?"

"Yeah."

"Well, thank you for coming by and introducing yourself to me."

"Well, I came by for something else too," he disclosed, and she raised an eyebrow again to hear more. "I was wondering if you could spot me a loan?"

"Sure. What do you need?"

"Twenty dollars would be great."

"Sure. No problem," she expressed, moving behind the desk, and retrieving her purse from the cabinet, just as Parker entered from the back room.

"Parker, my man!" Frankie addressed.

"Hi, Frankie," he welcomed as they bumped fists.

Vinny handed Frankie the twenty dollars. "Thanks, sis," he acknowledged. "Gotta jet. Talk soon." She nodded as he turned to leave. "Parker, catcha later, my man."

"Sure," Parker finalized as Frankie scurried out the door. "Vinny, you probably don't remember, but you said you weren't going to give him any more money."

"I did?"

"Yeah. You and your mother decided to make Frankie stand on his own two feet."

"He looks pathetic."

"He *is*, but that's not *your* problem."

****

"Hi, baby," Shelby chimed, strolling into an exquisite, ocean-front beach house and into Mayor Jackson Carson's arms, as he met her at the door, with his almond-tanned skin in contrast to her ivory complexion. He was dressed in black pants and a white, button-down shirt. His suit jacket and tie were lying on a side chair.

They kissed long and passionately, and he whispered in her ear, "Hi, beautiful." They kissed again. "I missed you."

"I missed you too," she made known, and they kissed again. "I saw you on tv today."

Breaking away, he snapped in his deep baritone voice, "Those damn reporters won't leave me alone."

Sitting on the couch and kicking off her heels, she declared, "Because you're so damn handsome."

"Wow! Thank you," he jeered, pulling her up in a big kiss again. He proceeded to unbutton her blouse. "Let's take a long, hot shower together."

"Um. That sounds wonderful," she agreed. They immersed themselves in kissing again, and he raised her skirt and sat on the couch, pulling her in a straddle across his lap. She moaned aloud as they kissed wildly. "I thought you wanted to take a shower."

"We will," he moaned in her ear. "*Later*."

****

"How was your session with the doctor today?" Chaz asked his wife over dinner.

"It was good. She's amazingly easy to talk to," she shared, eating the food she bought from a Mexican restaurant on her way home.

"That's good, sweetie."

"She said I shouldn't tell too many people about the flashback of the murder. It might put me in danger."

"She's right. Maybe we shouldn't tell too many people that you're seeing her at all."

"I think that's a good idea," she agreed then changed the subject. "Frankie came by the studio today to borrow money."

"You didn't give him any, did you?"

"I did," she admitted shyly. "I didn't remember that I shouldn't."

Laughing, he disclosed, "You probably would've given it to him even if you had remembered."

"Am I a push-over for my little brother?" she laughed with him.

"Somewhat," he revealed, getting up and putting his dishes in the dishwasher.

"I'll clean up. Go and take your shower."

"Okay, honey. I *am* tired," he expressed, then yawned and kissed her forehead before walking out.

Vinny sat at the table, staring into space, and feeling very nervous. Her hands were getting very moist with beads of sweat, and they were even beginning to shake a little. She couldn't understand why she felt so nervous when she thought about intimacy with her husband. She knew she had to try sooner or later. Dr. Bruce was right. Chaz might start looking elsewhere for love.

****

Shelby walked into a large, two-story, four-thousand-square-foot, white, frame house, combing through the mail she retrieved from her mailbox. "Hi, honey," a man entered the foyer in black, silk pajamas and a matching robe.

"Hi," she replied, meeting him with a quick kiss.

"You're late."

"Yeah, with Valencia's upcoming show, I'll have many late nights."

"Hungry?"

"No. I had a sandwich," she replied, thinking about her take-out lasagna with her handsome lover in their hide-a-way beach house.

"Oh, I see," he accepted, thinking," *You lying huzzy.*

"I'm going to take a shower. I'm beat," she shared, exiting.

"Shelby," called the medium-height man with a reddened face, balding gray hair, and a slight, protruding belly.

"Yes, honey," she acknowledged, swirling back to face her husband.

"What's going on?"

"What'd you mean? You know Valencia's show's coming up?"

"I'm not talking about that," he countered. "I'm talking about your distance lately."

"Tony, you know how consumed I get with these shows," she defended. "I don't have time for any hassles with you."

"I don't mean to hassle you. I just miss my wife."

"After the show, we'll have time to spend together. I promise," she lied, thinking that she had to cool it a little with Jackson until after the show.

"I love you, Shelby."

"And I love you," she stressed. "I'm just busy right now. Maybe after the show, we can take a trip or something."

"That would be nice."

She smiled wide, planted a kiss on his cheek, and added, "Then it's a date." As Shelby walked out, she couldn't help but think about Mayor Jackson Carson and how sexy he was. She could never give him up, even if it meant losing her husband and ending a fifteen-year marriage. She didn't want to hurt Tony. He's a good man, but she was in love with Jackson. He stirred up feelings in her that she didn't know existed. How could she give that up?

****

Chaz was in the warm, soothing shower remembering how Vinny and he used to shower together. He thought of their long walks together on the beach. He loved her so much. He began wondering if she would ever be his wife again, when suddenly, the shower door opened, and she stepped in with him. "May I join you, Doc?"

"Absolutely," he excitedly agreed, pulling her in his arms. They kissed long and hard as the water soothed their clinging bodies. "I love you so much."

"I love you too," she admitted, and he froze. He had been wanting to hear those words from his wife's lips for weeks now. Then he pulled her close. Their lovemaking was breathtaking, and it was hard for them to release each other.

When they finally made it to the bed, he rolled on her, kissing her passionately. "I thought you were tired," she teased.

"Not anymore," he whispered in her ear, and she smiled wide. "Are you tired, baby?"

"Not at all," she whispered back.

Their love knew no boundaries as they explored each other's body as if it was the first time. When the explosion erupted again, they clanged to each other so sweetly until every ounce of their desires were satisfied. Then they snuggled close in each other's arms and drifted off to sleep together. Chaz was so happy to have his wife back. Vinny was kicking herself because she had waited so long to experience something so beautiful with her husband. She was thankful that he was so patient with her.

Chapter 5

"What happened? You look different somehow," Dr. Bruce inquired of Vinny as they sat in her office.

Vinny chuckled, "What'd you mean?"

"Vinny..." she singsong. "What happened?" She paused for a moment, examining her patient. "Oh, I see."

"You see *what*?" she laughed, squirming in her seat, noticing the warmth of the soft fabric in hunter-green slacks and a crème-colored, silk blouse on her skin. She cocked her head to one side, feeling the pressure of the huge, dangling, hoop, white-gold earrings.

"Were you finally able to be intimate with your husband?"

Blowing hard, Vinny blurted out, "Yes, and it was *wonderful*!"

"That's great."

"I don't know why I was so scared. He is so patient and so kind."

"Did it feel familiar to you?"

"You know, now that you mentioned it, it did. It felt *remarkably familiar*."

"Have you had any more visions?"

Shaking her head, she grunted, "Ump um. Just that one."

"How is work going?"

"Great. I'm painting steady, and Parker is a jewel. I don't know what I would've done without him."

"I'm glad you're settling back into your life."

"I still can't remember anything."

"Let's go back to your vision."

"All right."

"Close your eyes, Vinny."

Vinny searched for confirmation, "Close my *eyes*?"

"Yes. Humor me," Dr. Bruce replied, and she hunched her shoulders and complied. "Go back to that vision. Think hard. Vinny." She paused. "See the person falling." She paused to give Vinny time to obey. "Now, go backward. See that falling body in reverse. Can you see it?"

"A little," she squeezed out.

"Keep trying, Vinny. Try to see the person's face."

"It's too dark," she whined. "I can only see red. He has on a red shirt."

"So, it's a *he*?"

"Yeah. I think so. I don't see long hair."

"Is he young or old?"

"He's….young, I think." she grumbled.

"Okay, Vinny, that's enough. Open your eyes."

"I'm sorry. I can't remember much."

"No problem. You did great," the patient doctor encouraged. "Vinny, how do you feel about hypnosis?"

****

"Hi, Parker," Shelby greeted, walking into the studio in her short, black, flare rayon skirt with a matching blouse, wide red belt, and three-inch, black heels. Her silky, blonde hair was dazzling in soft curls and a red barrette securing it on the left side.

He looked up from polishing a gold frame and acknowledged, "Hi, Shelby. How are you?"

"Wonderful," she glowed in her own perky style. "Where's Valencia?"

"Not here," he answered dryly with a perfect smile and a burgundy du-rag covering the soft curls on his head, wearing blue denim, sleeveless painter's overalls, and exposing medium-sized tattoos on his shoulder.

"When is she coming back?"

He sing-song, "Don't know."

"Do you have any pieces ready for me to see?"

"You'll have to wait for Vinny," he stated, stopping with his polishing, and focusing on her. "You know she doesn't allow anyone to look at her work before it's finished."

Lighting a cigarette, she affirmed, "Not *Valencia's* pieces...*yours*!"

His eyes widened as he solicited, "You want to see *my* work?"

"Yes. Valencia's including some of your pieces in the show, right?"

Smiling wide, he granted, "Sure. Back here. Follow me, Princess."

****

"Do you think hypnosis will help me remember."

"No guarantees, but it could," answered Dr. Bruce.

Vinny took a deep breath and responded, "Can I talk to my husband about it first?"

"Of course. No hurry," she clarified. "Hypnosis can sometimes do wonders to help people remember their past."

"Sounds dangerous."

"How so?"

Fidgeting in her chair, she replied, "I don't know. I guess I've seen too many bad movies about hypnosis." She laughed and Dr. Bruce smiled with her.

"It's up to you. No pressure," the doctor explained. "A minute ago, when you closed your eyes, you seemed to be relaxed enough to remember a little. Hypnosis will allow you to further relax your mind to hopefully bring the memories to the surface."

"I would *love* to remember. I feel so frightened all the time."

"I understand," the doctor urged. "Are there certain times when you feel more frightened than other times?"

"The only time I feel totally free is when I'm painting."

"That's interesting," Dr. Bruce acknowledged. "Let's pick up from there next time, okay?"

****

"Frankie, I hope you're not coming here for money again! I told you not to *ever* come to my job again for money!" his mother charged into her son as soon as he entered the restaurant.

"No, I didn't come for money, Ma!" he retaliated, trying not to yell.

She blew hard to calm down and added, "I told you. I won't give you any more money. Get a job, Frankie."

"I will. I just came to tell you that Justine called and said she's coming home," he shared then walked off.

"I know she's coming home. I talked to her. The semester is almost over," she acknowledged. Patrice Dow took a deep breath. She felt so disappointed in her son. He was twenty-five years old and doing absolutely *nothing* with his life.

"Good afternoon, Patrice," a deep, baritone voice spoke, and she turned.

"Good afternoon, Mayor," she recognized. "How are you?"

"I'm well. Thank you," he replied, standing at six-feet, one-inch, with almond-tanned, smooth skin, and a winning smile. His tailor-made suit fit him perfectly. His temple-gray, short-cut, groomed, wavy-black hair added sophistication to his fifty-eight years. "So, what's good today?"

"*Everything* is good," she chuckled, showing him and his two aids, doubling for bodyguards, a table. Since Mayor Jackson Carson has been cracking down on crime, he has been getting numerous death threats, so the city made sure he was protected with two aids who could also serve as bodyguards because of their military backgrounds. "Here, have a seat. Your waitress will be right over." Since Patrice was already seating them, the hostess quietly walked away.

As they sat, he asked, "How is your daughter. I hear she's having memory problems?"

"Yeah, she is, but she's doing okay."

"Is the show still on?" asked Liam, one of the aids, in his deep-routed Italian heritage accent. Liam Rossi was a five-foot-ten-inch, muscular-built man with smooth, jet-black hair. His etched features were characteristic of his heritage, which he proudly flaunted.

"Yes, it sure is," answered Patrice, as a waitress approached.

"I have some of Vinny's paintings," Mayor Carson announced. "She's very talented."

"Yes, she is," she acknowledged. "Thank you for supporting her."

"I know she's upset about not being able to remember," Elijah added. Elijah James was the other bodyguard. He was as tall as the mayor with a shaved bald head and a medium-length thick beard. His teeth were crooked with a big gap in the front. His uneven, chocolate skin was due to eczema and a major concern for him, which is why he grew the beard.

"Yes, she is, but she's coping," Patrice answered. "Well, gentlemen, enjoy your meal."

"Thank you, Patrice," Mayor Carson concluded. "We'll be at the show."

"Thank you. I know that would please Vinny," she finalized, walking away, as the waitress stepped forward to take their orders. Patrice hoped her daughter would be ready for her big event.

****

"Shelby stopped by. She looked at some of my pieces," Parker announced to Vinny when she entered the back room.

"What did she say? Is she going to handle your career?"

"She didn't say, but she did say my pieces were impressive," he shared.

"Wow, that's great, Parker! For an art manager to say *impressive*, you're on your way, kiddo!" she cheered, grabbing him in a big bear hug.

"Thank you, Vinny," he shared her enthusiasm. "I owe it all to you."

She sarcastically joked, "*You* had a *little* to do with it." They laughed together. "You're talented, Parker! I'm so proud of you!" They hugged again.

He felt so blessed to be working for Vinny. She was like a big sister to him. She wasn't threatened by his success. What a gal! If she wasn't married, he would probably marry her himself…or at least *try*.

****

"How is her memory?" the person with the snake pinky ring asked over the telephone. "Does she have it back yet?"

"No," Frankie answered, sitting in the bar drinking a beer. "I saw her. She ain't getting no memory back."

"I have to tell you; I'm getting extremely nervous. I know she's your sister, but I don't like loose ends."

"I understand that, but I would tell you if she was getting her memory back. I have just as much to lose as you do!"

"Make sure you remember that!" the person snapped. "Your sister will *not* be the end of me!"

****

"Chaz, I'm leaving," Monica announced, poking her head in his office door, swinging her long, weaved hair out of her face.

"Okay. Have a nice evening," he responded, barely looking up at her, and that disappointed her. She was hoping that he would notice her thighs in her short dress and high-heeled sandals.

She disappointedly turned quickly and bumped into a medium-built white lady with short, curly brown hair with a few gray streaks in the front. "Hi, Monica."

"Oh, hi Brooke," the young woman responded. "Sorry. I didn't see you."

"No problem."

"See you tomorrow."

"I won't be here tomorrow," Brooke shared, brushing her A-lined, rush-colored, below-the-knee dress down. Brooke Myers was forty-five years old with a set of twins in college, one boy and one girl. She met and married her husband immediately after graduating from high school. He is an African American man who went into the military while she went to college. Her short-cut, brown hair made her look younger than she was. "I'll be at a curriculum meeting at the DO." Brooke smiled sweetly, and Monica flashed her a quick smirk which served as a smile, and she was gone.

"Hi, Brooke," Chaz spoke, sitting at his desk. "Come in."

"Hi, Chaz," she replied, entering his office, and closing the door.

"Ah, this must be serious," he joked, turning his attention to the modestly dressed woman as she sat in front of his desk. "What's up?"

"Monica!"

"Oh!" he acknowledged. "What about her?"

"Chaz, we have a dress code here. Why is she allowed to wear those seductive, see-through, show-all, short outfits, when we hound the kids and teachers for the same, and even send them home for doing so?"

"Because her uncle is on the school board," he chuckled.

"Not funny, Chaz," she held her ground, and he sobered quickly. "Do *we* run this school or the *board*."

He took a deep breath then promised, "I'll talk to her."

"If you don't feel comfortable talking to her, I will," she offered. "I would've done so, but I wanted to talk to you first."

"That would be great if you would talk to her, but you won't be here tomorrow."

"I'll be here Monday."

"You want to wait that long?"

"Not really."

He took another deep breath then confirmed, "I'll talk to her tomorrow." He chuckled and added as she stood, "You know this isn't going to end well."

She added, "You can handle it. She thinks the sun rises and sets on you."

"What?" he gurgled.

"Oh, don't play innocent, *mister*!" She burst into laughter. "You know that girl has eyes for you!"

"That's crazy!"

"Crazy or not, you need to keep her at arm's length."

"Thanks for the warning."

"*Men*!" she spat jovially as she turned to leave. "So *naïve*!"

****

Vinny walked out of the studio at dust dark while Parker locked the door. "Where did you park?" he asked, hopping on his huge motorcycle.

"Across the street," she answered, pointing to her brand-new, blue Lexus. "I couldn't find a park when I returned from the doctors, and I hate parking garages."

"Oh, okay. I'll wait until you reach your car."

"See you tomorrow," she acknowledged as she proceeded across the street. Suddenly, Parker noticed a car barreling down the street, headed straight for Vinny.

****

"Hi, baby," Jake spoke, standing outside of Diamond's condominium door when she came home.

"Jake, what're you doing here?" she requested, carrying a bag from a Chinese restaurant.

"I wanted to see you. I enjoyed being with you again."

"Whoa, slow your roll, big boy!" she laughed. "That was a *one*-time thing!"

"You can't be *serious*!" he yelped, following her into the condo.

"Jake, I'm *very* serious. I haven't forgiven you yet," she made known, putting the bag of food on the counter.

"Did you get enough food for two?"

"I suppose so," she considered, kicking off her heels, and removing the food, paper plates, and plastic utensils from the bag.

"May I have my key back?" he probed as they washed their hands in the kitchen sink, then sat at the island to eat.

"No."

"Come on, baby, you can have my house keys back, too."

"I don't *want* your house keys back," she confirmed as they ate.

"Why, baby. I told you I was sorry for what I did."

"And that's supposed to make it right, Jake?!" she stressed, raising her voice a little. "You *hurt* me! I can't just forget that!"

He dropped his head momentarily, then raised it and asked, "What can I do to make this right?"

"Nothing!" she confirmed. "*If* I *ever* trust you again, it's gonna take *time*, and you can't *rush* it."

****

"Vinny!!!" Parker shouted, hopping off his bike, rushing to her, and with one move, swooping her up around the waist and diving to the ground, barely escaping the speeding car swishing by. "Are you alright?!"

A vision flashed before Vinny's eyes, and she could see the face of a young, light-brown African American man in a red, hooded shirt and sagging blue jeans, falling to the ground clutching his bloody chest. His hair was spiking on the top of his head in short twists with a red band encircling them. "Just scraped my hand on the pavement a little," she finally squeezed out of trembling lips, shaking her right hand. "But I'm okay. Thank you." She focused on his caring face and sparkling, clear hazel eyes. "You saved my life."

"That guy must be crazy!" he yelped, yanking his cell phone from his pocket. "I'm calling the police!"

****

Chaz sat on the couch, watching the television in black boxer shorts and a white T-shirt. He looked at his watch. "Where are you, Vinny?" he pondered. He took a breath then yanked up his cell phone from the coffee table and dialed.

"Hi," Vinny answered weakly, sitting in her studio while two policemen took Parker's statement.

"Honey, are you still at work?"

"Chaz, the police is here. There was an incident?"

"Accident?!" he gasped. "What kind of accident?"

"No, baby, an *incident*, not an *accident*," she clarified. "I'll tell you about it when I get there."

"I'm on the way."

"No, honey. We're finishing up here. I'm leaving in about five minutes."

"I'll come and get you."

"No, honey. I'm fine."

"What happened, baby?"

"I'll tell you everything when I get there."

"Baby…"

"I'm fine, honey. I promise."

"Are you sure?"

"Yes. I'm sure," she confirmed. "See you soon."

****

"Shelby?" her husband called as she entered their house, stepping out of her heels.

"Yes, Tony," she called back, as her husband met her in the foyer, rubbing his hand across his balding gray hair.

"Rough day?" he inquired, planting a kiss on her cheek, standing in a gray pajama set.

"No, just *busy*," she answered. "Have you started dinner?"

"Yeah. Hungry?"

"Starved. What did you cook?"

"Baked chicken breast, salad, and baked potato."

"Um, sounds delicious," she beamed. "I'll go and take a quick shower and be right back." She started out the door. "How was work?"

"Not bad. I got two new patients today. The cutest little puppies you've ever seen." he chuckled.

"Being a vet, I bet you see a lot of cute animals."

"I do," he agreed, as she walked away. "Hurry, the food is almost ready."

"Okay," she called back as her cell phone blasted, while he exited back into the kitchen. She noticed Jackson Carson's cell phone number on her caller ID, so she picked it up quickly as a wide smile enveloped her face. "Hey."

"Hey," he spoke softly, sitting on the couch in his den. "What're you doing?"

"Just got home. What're you doing?" She closed her bedroom door and flopped on the bed.

"Thinking about you," he cooed.

"That sounds good," she purred, lying on the bed, basking in the warmth of his strong, sexy voice.

"Meet me."

"Baby, I just got home. Tony's gonna know something's up if I go out again tonight."

"Something *is* up," he flirted, and she chuckled.

"You're so bad!"

"What time can you meet me at the beach house in the morning?"

"Early."

"Good," he replied as he heard his wife approaching. "See you in the morning. Love you."

"Love you," she concurred before hanging up. Shelby felt like a teenager whenever she either heard Jackson's voice or saw his handsome face. He just made her feel warm and fuzzy all over. She loved him, but she didn't want to hurt Tony because he's a good man, and a good husband to her. Not too many men would work all day, come home, and cook. She knew *Jackson* wouldn't, but she loved him. If she could get him to leave his wife, she would leave her husband in a snap. But she knew Jackson would never get a divorce, not because he loved his wife so much but because he wanted to run for governor one day and maybe even senator. She took a deep breath. Shelby didn't know how much longer she could live like this, *loving* one man and *living* with another.

****

"Who was that?" a petite, light-brown woman asked Jackson. She had straight, shoulder-length, brownish hair and was wearing a long, white night shirt with fuzzy, white slippers.

"Elijah," he lied.

"You said *love you*."

"What?" he questioned, stalling for time to think of a lie.

"You said *love you*. Do you tell Elijah you *love him*?" She sat beside him.

"Oh, no!" he exploded in laughter. "I said love *it*! Elijah was sharing a plan to stop the violence in town."

"The *violence*?"

"Yeah, honey. You know we've been under a lot of pressure to come up with a plan to stop all the violence in town."

"Oh," she understood. "What's the plan?"

"Honey, I don't feel like discussing that tonight," he expressed, yawning. "I'm bushed. I'm going to bed." He planted a quick kiss on her cheek then stood. "Good night." He left quickly before she could ask any more questions, as he thought, *That was close. I gotta be more careful in the future.*

****

"Are you sure I can't stay the night?" Jake asked, standing at Diamond's door with her.

"Yes, I'm sure," she confirmed.

"May I see you tomorrow?"

"Let's take a break."

"Diamond, I love you. I want to be with you."

She opened the door and replied, "Yeah *whatever*!"

"*Excuse* me!"

"Six months ago, you loved *Angela*!"

"I told you I made a mistake."

"So, you said," she recognized sarcastically.

"You're never going to forgive me. Are you?"

"I don't know, Jake. All I know is that I'm very tired, and I want to go to bed," she stressed.

"I could massage your feet," he cooed, moving close to her, and she laughed. "What's so funny?"

She shook her head and replied, "Nothing." He stared at her as she sobered. "*Tomorrow*, Jake. We'll talk *tomorrow*!" She stepped back. "Good night."

****

"Babe, what happened?" Chaz immediately charged into Vinny as soon as she walked into the house, where he had already opened the door for her.

"I was almost hit by a hit-and-run car."

"What?! Did you see who it was?!"

"No. It was too fast. Parker saw more than I did. He pulled me out the way."

"Thank God for Parker," he breathed, pulling her in his arms. He released her immediately, staring into her eyes. "Are you all right?"

"Yeah, just a little bruised hand."

"Thank God," he praised, pulling her in his loving arms again.

When he finally let her go, she took a short breath and shared, "Chaz, I had another flashback."

"Really?" he bade, guiding her to sit at the kitchen table. "What did you see?"

"A young black man. He was probably in his twenties, light-brown skin with twists in his hair and a red headband," she explained.

"Did you tell the police?"

"No."

"Why not, honey? What if that car was intentionally trying to hit you? Someone might think you know something about the murder."

"But I didn't see the person who shot him."

"Honey, they don't know that. They might think you did," he hypothesized. "Baby, you could be in danger."

Chapter 6

"You tried to *kill* her?!" Frankie fumed in his cell phone, sitting on his bed. "I told you she don't remember *nothing*!"

"Well, I gotta protect *myself*!"

"So, are you gonna try that shit again?"

"No. It was just a warning."

"A *warning*? Now she'll have her guard up, and not to mention the *police*!"

"She called the police?"

"Of course, she did! You tried to *kill* her!"

"Make sure you let me know if she starts to remember anything because if you don't, *you'll* be in the morgue with *her*," the person warned. "The next time, *I won't miss*!"

****

"Do you think you could recognize the person you saw in your flashback?"

"I think so," Vinny answered Dr. Bruce, sitting in front of her in the doctor's office. "Do you think I should tell the police?"

"It's up to you. What do you think?"

"I don't know."

"Did you talk it over with your husband?"

"Yes. He thinks I should."

"Then why haven't you?"

"Because I can't remember! I don't wanna sound like a fool in front of the police!"

"Have you talked to your husband about hypnosis?"

"Not yet. After what happened last night, it wasn't on my mind."

"Understandable," the doctor acknowledged. "Vinny, you might want to do something soon. If you witnessed a murder, that car that almost hit you was probably no accident." She took a breath as Vinny pondered what the doctor was saying. "They could try again."

****

"Mom!"

"Justine?!" her mother shrieked, running in from the kitchen with an apron on, drying her hands. "Hello, honey!" Patrice Dow hugged her daughter tight, as Frankie strolled in slowly with his hands in his pockets.

"Hi, big brother," Justine spoke, exposing a deep dimple on each of her cheeks, with long, micro-braids hanging almost to her waist. Her black tights caressed her curves with a long black and white flowered blouse accenting her short, one hundred forty pounds. Like her sister Vinny, much of her weight settled on her hips and thighs with no visible protruding stomach.

"What's up?" Frankie greeted his sister, then hugged her slightly with a gentle pat on her back. "How is the family nurse?"

"*Future* nurse," Justine chuckled. "Don't jinx me."

"Ah, you got this!" he laughed with her. "Ma, anything to eat?"

"I'm cooking *now*," his mother responded as a young man with a short, neat haircut entered with two suitcases.

"Just drop them there," Justine instructed.

"Hi, Ryan," Mrs. Dow acknowledged.

"Hi, Mrs. Dow," Ryan responded, giving her a quick kiss on the cheek. He was a tall, slinky figure, wearing neatly pressed blue jeans and a white button-down shirt hanging loosely. "I have a few more things to get out the car."

"Frankie, would you please help Ryan," Mrs. Dow suggested.

"What happened. Y'all got kicked outta school?" Frankie laughed, heading towards the door.

"No, silly," Justine chuckled. "We exempted our exams, so we could leave early."

"Impressive," her brother admired.

"Yes, it is," Mrs. Dow agreed. "Come on in the kitchen with me, honey. I have pots on the stove." Her daughter followed her.

"Where's dad?" Justine inquired.

"Working."

"Oh, that's right. It's still early."

"Yes, it is. I got off early today so I could cook you something good to eat."

"Oh, that's sweet, Ma," she raved, sitting on the stool around the island in the kitchen, while her mother attended to the pots on the stove. "So, what's this with Vinny? Can she remember yet?"

"Not yet. Have you talked to her?"

"No. I haven't called her yet. I figured she wouldn't remember me, and it would feel weird."

"I haven't seen her since she left the hospital," Mrs. Dow explained. "Well, she'll meet everyone at our Sunday dinner."

"I can't wait for our Sunday dinner. I missed it."

"We missed having you, sweetie...*and* Vinny."

"I'm looking forward to seeing grandma," she shared, pushing her long braids behind her ear, and dropping a peanut in her mouth on her light-brown face. "I hope Vinny's all right. She must be scared to death."

****

Vinny strolled out of Dr. Bruce's office, deep in thought. She walked into the parking garage searching for her car. Suddenly, she heard footsteps behind her, and she stopped, but the sound ceased. She took a deep breath then proceeded her stride, and the footsteps invaded her thoughts again. She grew frightened and quickened her steps into a slow trot to her car, and the footsteps quickened behind her. "Help!" she yelled as she ran faster. Suddenly, she turned the corner and crashed into someone, and she released a wail of hysterical, earth-shattering, eardrum-rupturing screams.

****

"Are you still scheduling Vinny's show?" Shelby's husband asked, sliding into bed with her, while she was sitting up, chatting on her laptop with Mayor Jackson Carson.

"Yeah, we're gonna try," she answered her husband, quickly saying goodnight to her lover, and putting her laptop away.

"Is her memory coming back?"

"Not yet."

"Then how are you going to have a show?"

"Tony, she still knows how to paint."

"Really?"

"Yes. Valencia is very talented. She hasn't forgotten how to create beautiful paintings."

"That's good," he acknowledged. "It's funny how the mind works."

"Yes, it is. She still can't remember anything, but she's painting better than ever."

He took a deep breath then asked cautiously, "So, do you think she'll ever remember what *you* did?"

****

"Mrs. Perkins, it's me!" the man yelled, trying to settle Vinny. "It's Marvin, the security guard." Vinny gradually calmed down and focused on the man.

She blew hard, slumped, and recognized, "Marvin?!" She settled, letting out another deep breath. "I'm sorry."

"No problem. I heard you yell *help*," he explained. "What's wrong?"

"Did you see anyone following me?"

"No, ma'am," he answered. "Come on, let me show you to your car." He picked her purse and keys off the ground and handed them to her. "Are you alright?"

She took another breath, receiving her purse and keys, and established, "Yes, I'm fine. Thank you."

The person with the snake pinky ring slid quietly behind a brick column in the garage.

****

"Hey. Where are you?" Justine asked over her cell phone, standing in her room with a three-inches-above-the-knee, flare, blue jean skirt on, sandals with six-inch heels, off-the-shoulder, waist-length, tan blouse, and her micro-braids in a neat ponytail. "The movie will be starting soon."

"Listen, baby, mom wants me to help her get some things out of the attic for the church garage sale," Ryan explained.

"Can't you do that tomorrow?"

"She's working tomorrow, and she has to take the things to the church tonight, so they will have them for the garage sale in the morning."

"Ryan, that's a lame excuse!" she snapped. "I'm dressed already. Why do you have to go to the church with her?"

"She has a lot of stuff, baby. She can't take all of it by herself. I'll make it up to you, baby. I promise."

"How, Ryan?! How are you going to make it up to me?!" She was yelling now.

"We can go to the movies tomorrow."

"Forget it, Ryan!" she snapped, hanging up her cell phone and throwing it on the bed just as her mother was about to enter her bedroom.

"Wow! Somebody's in trouble!" Patrice yelped.

"Oooh!" she groaned. "He makes me so mad!"

"He can't come tonight?"

"His *mommy* wants him to do something, so what else is new?" she complained, and her mother chuckled.

"Be patient, honey," her mother suggested. "Change your clothes, come and watch tv with your dad and me."

Justine took a deep breath, nodded, and agreed, "All right but one day Ryan is gonna go too far...he *and* his *mother*!"

****

"How are you, Vinny?" Diamond asked, sitting in Vinny's kitchen with her friend.

Taking a breath, Vinny confessed, "Not good. I think I'm getting paranoid now."

"Why? What happened?"

"I attacked the security guard at my therapist's building today."

"What?!" she shrieked.

"I thought someone was following me, so I yelled and when Marvin, the security guard, came to help me, he scared the mess outta me," she explained.

"Oh, honey, I'm sorry."

"Marvin was cool though."

"That's good. Is there anything I can do?"

Vinny drew another breath. "Yes. Tell me about *anything* in my life that you can tell me. Tell me about our friendship," Vinny suggested. "I mean, we seem so different."

"Sure. I can do that," Diamond cheerfully answered, swishing her long blonde hair behind her back. "My mom and I moved here when I was in junior high. We were trying to get away from my abusive dad. In trying to beat information out of my mother's brother, he almost killed him and was sentenced to five years in jail. You and I started talking, and you shared with me that your father was in prison for life for murdering his wife, so we bonded."

"Wait! Wait! Wait! Did you say my *father* is in *prison*?!"

"Yeah, what of it?"

"My mother and father visited me at the hospital!"

"Oh, no, honey. Mr. Dow is your *stepfather*. Your mother and father never married. After your mother married Mr. Dow, she had your brother Frankie and your sister Justine," Diamond explained then took a sip of her iced tea.

"This is so strange," she pondered as they heard the front door open.

"Honey!" Chaz called.

"In the kitchen!" Vinny made known then stood and met him with a kiss.

"Hi, baby," he greeted her.

"Hi," she responded, and they kissed again.

"Hi, Diamond," he added.

"Chaz," she welcomed.

"I'm going to take a shower, sweetheart," he announced, and Vinny nodded.

After he was gone, she sat at the table again with her friend, and Diamond probed, "How are things with you two?"

Smiling wide, she answered, "Great!"

"Fabulous!" her friend acknowledged. "You're blessed."

"I agree," she accepted then decided to change the subject back to what they were discussing. "What do you do?"

"I'm in advertising."

"I can see that," Vinny recognized. "You're so stylish."

"Thankyouverymuch!" she chuckled. "As a matter of fact, I just made partner!"

"Partner!" Vinny yelped. "That's wonderful!"

"Yeah, I think so," she snickered. "Our banquet is next Saturday. I hope you and Chaz can come."

"Sure. We'll be there."

Well, I better get outta here, so you can relax with your husband." Diamond stood, and Vinny stood with her.

"Thank you for coming over."

"Are you kidding?!" Diamond joked. "You're my girl!" They hugged as Chaz entered in some sweatpants and a sleeveless muscle shirt.

"I'll get dinner," Vinny announced.

He nodded and suggested, "I'll see Diamond out." Vinny nodded, moving to the stove.

"I'll call you tomorrow," Diamond promised as she left.

Chaz opened the front door for Diamond and walked out with her. "Does she remember what happened between *us*?"

"No."

"Are you going to tell her?"

"Why would I do that?"

"It might help her remember."

"I doubt that."

"Okay. If you say so. Goodnight."

"Goodnight, Diamond," he finalized as Vinny joined him at the door and waved to her friend. Chaz caught Vinny's hand, and they entered the house together.

"So, what's her story?" she inquired jovially.

"What'd you mean?" he chuckled.

"Is she as nice as she seems?"

Bursting into laughter, he teased, "No you didn't!"

"Well?" she inquired, laughing with him.

"You and Diamond have been friends a long time," he shared, sitting at the table, as she fixed their plates. "She's nice but she does love to *play* a little too much sometimes."

"Has she ever come on to you?"

"Why would you ask that?"

"I don't know. Just something flirtatious about her."

"So, you think she would go after a married man?" he chuckled.

"Maybe."

"Honey, Diamond and you are as close as sisters. I don't think she would *ever* betray you."

"So, that's a *no*. She's never come on to you?"

He turned to her and stared her squarely in the eyes and announced very sternly, "No!" He took her hand as she stood at the table. "Even if she had, I would *never* cheat on you."

"Never?"

"*Never!*"

She rubbed her hand through her kinky hair roughly and shrieked, "Oh, I wish I could remember! I wish I could remember *everything*! This is so frustrating!"

"I know, baby," he understood. "Is Dr. Bruce helping at all?"

"A little," she answered, sitting at the table with him. "She suggested hypnosis. What'd you think about that?"

"Whew, *hypnosis*!" he chortled. "I don't know. What do you think?"

"Dr. Bruce thinks it might help me remember."

"Well, if it'll help, baby, maybe you should consider it."

She took a deep breath then hesitantly asked, "Would you take me to the place where my accident occurred?"

Chaz focused on his wife, placed his hand on hers, squeezed lovingly, and inquired softly, "Are you sure you're ready?"

"No," she shared. "But it's something I think I need to do." He nodded his understanding. "I'm so tired of being *afraid* all the time. I need to do whatever I can to start remembering." She took a breath. "Will you take me?"

"Sure, baby, of course, I'll take you. Tomorrow is Saturday. We have all day to do whatever you want," he concurred as the telephone began to ring. "I'll get it, sweetie."

He stood and picked up the telephone mounted on the wall. "Hello?"

"Hi, Chaz." Patrice Dow spoke on the other end of the telephone.

"Hi, Mama Pat. How are you?"

"I'm fine. How is Vinny?"

"She's okay."

"Hey, I don't want to hold you. I just wanted to see if you and Vinny are coming for dinner Sunday, so she can see her family."

"Wait a moment, Mama Pat," he held then focused on his wife. "Honey, this is your mother. Your family always have Sunday dinner at your parent's house. She wants to know if you feel up to coming this Sunday."

Vinny hunched her shoulders then replied, "Sure."

Back into the phone, he confirmed, "Mama Pat, we'll be there."

"Okay, honey. Great! About two?"

"Fine," he agreed. After Chaz hung up, he sat back at the table with his wife to finish his dinner.

"So, why didn't you tell me about my dad?"

"I didn't know if you were ready for that. Who told you, Diamond?" he inquired, and she nodded.

"Is he in prison here in town?'

"No. The prison is about an hour away."

"Do I ever go to see him?"

"Not much. He wasn't really in your life before he went to prison. Your mother had you when she was fifteen and he was twenty-five."

"Wow! Was it rape?"

"No, but it was statutory, so he did some time for it anyway," he explained.

"So, how old am I?"

"Thirty-two."

She thought for a moment then asked, "You said he *did* some time. Diamond said he's in prison now."

"He is but not because of the rape."

"Then why is he in prison now?"

"Baby, are you sure you want to hear all of this now?"

"Yes, I'm sure."

He took a breath and continued, "When he was released for the rape, a few years later, he married Shania. He came home one day from work early, and Shania was in bed with another man. Your father, Lance Greene, went to his barn, got his shotgun, and killed her in the house. By then the man had already gone. So, your father went to the man's house that night and shot him dead in front of his wife and three children. The judge said he had time to think about his actions. He was sentenced to life with no possibility of parole."

Vinny blew hard then came back with, "Whew! Thank you for not telling me that my *father* is a *murderer*."

Chapter 7

As Vinny stood with her husband on the edge of the road, looking down at the steep embankment where her car had plummeted down the twenty-five-foot shrubbery slope, she felt weak in the knees. "Are you all right, sweetheart?" he questioned her.

She squeezed out a shaky, "Why aren't I dead?"

"Oh, baby, it wasn't your time," he confirmed, placing his arm around her shoulders, and pulling her close. "And I thank God it wasn't."

"What was I doing way out here? Do you know?"

"I don't know, sweetie, but Shelby lives about two miles down that road," he replied, pointing.

"She does?"

He confirmed, "Yes. Maybe you were going to see her."

She took a deep breath. "I *wish* I could *remember*. Chaz, I feel so lost. I want my *memory* back," she whined, growing upset, and her husband pulled her in his arms lovingly and squeezed her tight while she cried in his chest. "I can't even remember going to school or getting married, or *anything*."

"It's okay, baby. You'll get your memory back," he sympathized with his wife.

"All my memories are...*gone*! I can't stand this!" she cried in her husband's caring arms. "All my memories are *forgotten*!"

"Baby, you're get them all back," her husband tried to comfort his hysterical wife. "And if you don't, we can make new ones! *Better* ones!"

Vinny pulled back and asked very weakly, "The doctor said all the swelling has gone down on my brain, and I should be able to remember. What could have happened so badly that would have me not *wanting* to remember?" She sniffed her tears back and took a deep breath. "What am I trying to block out?!"

****

"Whacha doing?" Justine asked Frankie, jumping on the porch chair beside him in Daisy Dukes denims, exposing a tattoo on the side of her left calf and on her back, right above her panty line, with a tan color, short, sleeveless blouse, exposing her belly button and another tattoo on her right shoulder down to her biceps.

"What's up, Nursey?"

"Not *yet*."

"Where're your clothes?" he teased, puffing on a cigarette.

"What're you talking about?! I'm *wearing* clothes!" she giggled.

He chuckled, "Yeah *right*!" She burst into laughter, and so did he.

"What're you, the *fashion* police?!" she continued to laugh, punching his arm.

"Ouch!"

Indicating his cigarette, she added, "You know those things will kill you."

"Well, we can't live forever."

"You're a nut," she laughed with her brother briefly then sobered. "Have you seen Vinny since the accident?"

"Yeah. I went by her studio."

"How is she?"

"She looks the same."

"I know she *looks* the same, dummy! Did she know you?"

"Hell no! She don't know her damn self!"

"That must be awful."

"Yeah, I guess it is," he agreed. "Where's your boo?"

"Who...*Ryan*?"

"How many boos do you have? Dag, girl!" he chuckled.

"He had to help his *mommy* with something this morning," she shared. "Mommy dearest always comes first."

"*Mommy dearest*!" he burst into laughter. "Girl, you stupid! Do I hear a little women rivalry?"

"No," she laughed with him. "I wouldn't win if there *was* a rivalry!" She blew hard. "He said he'll be over later though! We'll see!"

"Well, I wish he hurry up, so you can leave *me* the hell alone."

She got up, rubbed his face, and joked, "Am I bothering you, big brother?"

Pushing her hand away, he snickered, "Get outta here!" They laughed together as she sat again. "When y'all getting married?"

"*Married*?!" she screamed. "We have to finish school first! I have two more years!" She laughed and added, "I can see it now, on our honeymoon, Ryan, me and his *mother*."

Frankie really burst into laughter and replied, "Mrs. Henry ain't that bad, is she?"

"Yes. She is," Justine confirmed.

"As long as he make an *honest* woman outta you."

"You should talk," she sarcastically replied. "What're you doing with your life?"

"I'm surviving."

"How, Frankie? Are you still fooling around with that thug *Jarrick*?"

"None of your damn business!"

"Language!" Mrs. Dow shrieked, walking out of the house, onto the porch with her children. "Frankie, can you run to the store to get some milk?"

"Yeah, okay," he mumbled as a supped-up, red 70's Chevy pulled up in the yard.

"Speak of the devil," Justine yelped, as a medium-height young man jumped out the car and walked to the house with sagging blue jeans, an oversized, loosely hanging, blue shirt, and kinky locks in his hair on top of a pecan-tanned face.

Smiling wide, exposing fronts in his mouth, he greeted, "Hey, y'all!"

"My man!" Frankie returned the greeting with a hand slap.

"Hi, Jarrick," Mrs. Dow spoke. "How are you?"

"Hello, Mrs. D. I'm great. How are you?"

"I'm fine, Thank you."

"*Justine!*" Jarrick yelped. "You're looking *good*! When did you get home?"

"Hi, Jarrick," she frowned. "We're out for the summer."

"Where is the *boyfriend*?"

"He's around."

"Frankie, I need the milk right away," Mrs. Dow reminded.

"Okay, Ma."

"I'm going with you," Justine yelped, jumping up. "Let me get my purse."

Her mother called to her daughter as Justine rushed pass her into the house, "Put on some clothes first."

****

"Here is some hot tea, sweetie," Chaz offered, handing Vinny a cup while she sat on the couch with the television on but looking through their wedding photo album.

"Thank you."

"What's on the tube?"

"I don't know. I wasn't really paying attention."

Indicating her on a picture, he admired, "You looked so beautiful on our wedding day." She smiled sweetly at him.

"Our wedding was outside," she acknowledged.

"Yeah. In the park. It was beautiful."

"Yes, I see that it was."

He put his arm around her shoulders and checked lovingly, "Are you all right, honey?" She nodded slowly.

"You are so kind."

He smiled sweetly at her and declared, "I love you. I would do anything for you."

Their lips met gingerly. Their passions soared and their kisses grew more gropingly and aggressively. He swished her blouse off over her head, and she began unbuttoning his shirt. Suddenly, she froze, focusing on the television set. "What's wrong?" he breathlessly inquired.

Pointing to the television screen at a picture of a young, black man, she alleged, "That's *him*! That's the boy in my flashbacks that was shot."

Chaz turned the volume up, and the news anchor was asking for anyone with information on the murder of this young man named Kenneth Lewis, to contact the police immediately. "Are you sure?"

"Yes. That's *him*!" she insisted. "Oh my God!"

"The body was just found and identified," Chaz remarked.

"Should we call the police?"

"We don't know anything, baby. You didn't see the shooter. You don't even know where it occurred. I don't want to put you in danger until we have something more concrete, so the police will be able to find these people."

"Yeah, I guess you're right."

"Wait a minute. I just thought of something. Maybe the phone company can trace where your cell phone was at that time."

"My cell phone?" She was puzzled.

"Yes. It was never found at the wreckage. I bought you a new one."

"Sure. It's worth a try."

"I'll get on it Monday," he promised, eying her breasts in her black, lace bra, and licking his full lips. "Let's go to bed."

Chapter 8

Vinny, in a conservative, short-sleeved, deep purple, silk dress, sat in church beside Chaz, in a nice-fitting dark gray suit, listening to Pastor Donovan preach a sermon on *When You've Done All You Know to Do, Stand!* She felt a sense of peace at hearing those words. She knew she had to keep standing until she regained her memory. Her mother smiled at her from the choir stand, adorned in a black and gold robe, the same as the other choir members. Her stepfather sat proudly among the Deacons in a dark blue suit. Her Grandmother Eloise sat on the front row of pews, in a dark green suit with a black and dark-green bowl hat on her head, responding with an *Amen* to almost everything the Pastor said.

Although it felt good for Vinny to be in the presence of the Anointing, it felt strange because she didn't know anyone. She prayed silently to God to restore her memory before she lost her mind. Chaz seemed to be able to read her thoughts, so he took her hand and squeezed it gently.

After service, the Pastor came to Vinny and welcomed, "Vinny, it's good to see you." He was a caramel-tanned, medium-height man in his fifties, with salt and pepper, short, wavy hair. Vinny felt his smile was soothing and sincere.

"Thank you, Pastor," she accepted even though she had absolutely no recognition of either him or anyone else in the congregation who spoke to her so familiar after the service.

Extending a hand, Pastor Donovan recognized, "Chaz, nice to see you."

"Thank you, Pastor," he acknowledged. "I enjoyed the sermon."

"Thank you, brother. I give God all the Glory," the Pastor admitted then turned back to Vinny. "Hang in there, sister. God will fix it. Have Faith and don't get weary."

****

Diamond finished her makeup then checked herself in the mirror. She wondered if her straight, olive-colored dress was too short, which extended to the middle of her light-brown thighs. Her four-inch, strapless, tan sandals made her look taller and the dress shorter, but she thought she looked fine. Her bangs were suspended right above her eyebrows with her long, blonde, straight weaved hair, neatly flat-ironed down her back. She grabbed her purse and was about to leave when the doorbell rang. "Who could that be?" She yanked it open, and Jake was standing there smiling big, in a pair of blue jeans and a button-down, rust-colored shirt, hanging loosely. He was so tall, dark, and handsome, Diamond almost lost her breath. "Jake, what're you doing here?"

"Hi, baby. I wanted to see you. I thought maybe we could do something together today."

"I'm on my way out."

"You look beautiful."

"Thank you."

"When will you be back? I could wait for you."

"I don't know. I was invited to dinner at the Dows."

"Oh, Vinny's parents! They know me. I've been there with you before. May I come with you?"

"I don't know, Jake. They invited *me*."

"They wouldn't mind if I came with you," he hypothesized. "Please."

She took a deep breath then agreed, "Okay."

****

"Hey, big sis," Justine greeted Vinny at the door with a big hug, as Ryan trailed behind her.

Vinny smiled sweetly and replied, "Hi…"

"*Justine*," she finished, with her long braids in a ponytail, black tights, and an off-the-shoulder long, baby-blue silk blouse.

"I know you. I mean I know of you," Vinny acknowledged. "You are so cute."

"So are you," she chuckled. Admiring her sister in that yellow, knee-length, half-sleeved jumper, and a yellow band around her kinky-curly hair.

"I love the dimples," Vinny made known.

"Thank you," Justine accepted. "You always have." They hugged again. "Hi, brother-in-law."

"Hi, Justine. How is school?" Chaz greeted, hugging her.

"Great," she offered.

"You're out early."

"I exempted my finals, so I was able to leave early," she explained proudly.

"Awesome!" Chaz beamed, meeting her in a high-five.

"Vinny, Chaz, this is my boyfriend, Ryan Henry. Ryan, this is my sister, Vinny and her husband, Chaz. I mean *Dr*. Chazmond Perkins."

"*Chaz*, please," he offered. He and Ryan greeted each other with handshakes. "Nice to meet you, Ryan."

"Likewise, sir," he accepted.

"Hello, you two," Mrs. Dow spoke, entering from the kitchen in a lavender house dress and white apron. She hugged Vinny and Chaz as her husband entered also.

"Chaz," Mr. Dow greeted.

"Hello, Mr. Milo," Chaz responded, shaking his hand.

"Vinny, how are you, sweetheart?" Mr. Dow welcomed her with a hug.

"Hello," she acknowledged. Vinny felt so lost. None of these people, who were supposed to be her family, was familiar to her.

"Milo, take the kids in the den, please," his wife suggested. "Dinner will be ready soon."

"Sure," he agreed as Diamond opened the door.

"Hello, everyone!" she squealed in her own perky style, with Jake following close behind her.

****

"They found the body," the person with the snake pinky ring said over the telephone.

"I know. I heard."

"It's time to do something drastic before she remembers."

"I agree. I don't want to go to jail. What do you suggest?"

"We need to call our contacts in New York."

"You mean a *professional*?"

"Precisely."

"Do you think that's necessary?"

"I do."

"What is Frankie saying?"

"You know Frankie," the person said adjusting his pinky ring. "He's in denial, believing that she will never remember."

"Okay. Make the call. We can't wait around until she does."

"I agree. It's time we ended this and get rid of her...*now*!"

****

The huge table with the white, lace tablecloth was adorned with a good old-fashioned, Sunday dinner, which included collard greens, mashed potatoes, rice, brown gravy, green beans, dinner rolls, corn bread squares, macaroni and cheese, oxtails, fried chicken, baked chicken, country ham, pork chops, iced tea, fruit punch, and lemonade. The many desserts were still on the counter in the kitchen with banana pudding, strawberry shortcake, pecan pie, and ice cream in the freezer. Mr. Dow, at the head of the table, blessed the food before getting started. Frankie sat to the left of his father, with Diamond, Jake, and Grandma Eloise on the same side. Mrs. Dow sat at the head of the other side of the rectangular table with Vinny to the left of her, followed by Chaz, Justine, and Ryan. Mrs. Dow felt pleased that they had invested years ago in extending their dining room to make it bigger. They were able to add this large dining table that could hold all their children and guests every Sunday.

"Wow, Mrs. Dow, you outdid yourself," Diamond raved.

"Thank you, honey," she accepted. "I want all of you to enjoy yourselves. No dieting today." She focused on her confused daughter. "Vinny, have some mac and cheese. It's your favorite."

"Thank you," she received, retrieving the bowl from her mother to serve herself.

As the family talked, enjoying the wonderful meal Mrs. Dow prepared, Chaz leaned quietly to his wife and asked softly, "Are you all right?" Vinny focused on her husband, smiled politely, and nodded slightly. He then planted a soft kiss on her cheek. Diamond smiled sweetly at Chaz, and Vinny noticed the gesture and wondered what it was about. She wondered how friendly this pretty woman was with her husband. Was she *her* best friend or *his*?

"Mama, do you have enough?" Mrs. Dow inquired of her seventy-five-year-old mother, sitting to her right.

"If I eat anymore, I'll bust," Grandma Eloise chuckled. She was in great physical shape for her age in her small frame, a direct opposite from her daughter's plump physique. Her gray hair was in a neat bun, her brown pantsuit was stylish, and her makeup was modest. She still drove her own car and would come to dinner every Sunday with the family. "Vinny, how are you doing, sweetie?"

"Fine, thank you," Vinny responded to her grandmother friendly, even though she had no recollection of her, or *any* of them for that matter.

"We were hoping that getting with her family would help to bring back some familiarity to her," Mrs. Dow added, patting Vinny's shoulder lovingly.

Frankie looked up from his food at Vinny and asked cautiously, "Is it working?"

Shaking her head slightly, she whispered softly, "Not yet, but it certainly is a start."

"Bummer!" Frankie smirked.

"You look great, Vinny," added Jake.

"Thank you," she accepted.

"So, I guess I don't have to hide my candy jar anymore, since you don't remember how much you love candy," Grandma Eloise laughed.

"Oh, I still love candy," Vinny laughed with her.

"Are you seeing a therapist?" was Ryan's question.

"Yeah. Twice a week," she confirmed.

"Has your therapist suggested hypnosis?" Ryan continued. "I hear it does wonders to restore buried memories."

"As a matter of fact, she has," Vinny answered, and drew Frankie's attention. "I think we will try it soon."

"Is that what you're studying in college, Ryan?" was Diamond's question.

"Oh no. I'm an IT guy," Ryan chuckled. "Psychology is interesting though."

"Yes, it is," Chaz agreed. "I had to take a few psychology classes in education."

Justine laughed, "Has it helped with those bad ass kids?"

"It has, as a matter of fact," Chaz answered, laughing with her.

"Justine, watch that language!" her mother warned.

"Sorry, Mom."

Frankie was interested in that hypnosis his sister was thinking about trying, so he inquired, "Vinny, do you really think *hypnosis* will help you get your memory back?"

"I don't know, but I hope so," she answered. "I'm tired of living in the dark."

"I know that's right," Justine concurred.

"Hey, Ma, where is Michael?" Mrs. Dow asked her mother.

"Who knows," Grandma Eloise chuckled.

Mrs. Dow focused on Vinny and said, "Michael is your uncle, my younger brother. He lives with your grandma."

"You mean he lives *on* your grandma," Grandma Eloise snickered.

"How many kids does Uncle Michael have now?" questioned Justine.

"Three as I know of," her grandma replied. "Two boys and a girl, by three *different* women."

"Wow! Uncle Michael gets around!" Frankie laughed.

"And don't you go following in his footsteps," his mother warned.

"Ah, Ma. I know how to protect myself," he snarled.

"Um hum," Mrs. Dow groaned and decided to change the subject. "Dessert anyone."

As everyone mumbled how stuffed they were now, Frankie's mind was on that hypnosis his sister had talked about. He was worried because he knew that the moment she regained her memory, she was *dead*.

****

Shelby and Jackson lay in bed snuggled in each other's arms. "I could stay like this forever," Shelby cooed.

"So could I."

"Baby, do you think you could ever divorce Tammie?" she asked, and he held up over her on one elbow.

"I don't know, honey. You know my situation. I want to run for governor. A divorce wouldn't be good politics. I'm almost sixty years old. I can't afford to start over," he explained. "I thought we had an understanding."

"We do, sweetie, but I'm not getting any younger either. I'll be forty-nine in September. I just want us to be together. I love you."

"Baby, I love you, too," he confessed. "Can't we go on loving each other like we are?" He planted a kiss on her lips. "Can't we, baby?" Their kisses grew deep and passionate, as he slid on her. "I love you."

"I love you," she purred, receiving her lover for another round of satisfying bliss. Soon she forgot all about their conversation. She just wanted him in her life, no matter how brief.

****

"I enjoyed today at the Dows," Jake announced to Diamond as they entered her condo. "Thank you for letting me tag along."

"Sure," she recognized, and he pulled her in his arms in a warm embrace and kissed her lips sweetly.

"Can I stay?" he asked, kissing her again, and she nodded. "May I have my key back?"

She burst into laughter and warned, "Don't push it, big boy!" He might have forgotten about how he hurt her, but she hadn't. She wasn't sure if she could *ever* trust him again.

****

"Did anything seem familiar at dinner today?" Chaz asked Vinny, joining her on the couch in his boxer shorts, while she curled up in his arms in a short nightshirt.

"No. *Nothing*."

Pulling her closer in his arms, he assured, "Don't worry, baby. It'll be all right."

"I think I'm gonna let Dr. Bruce hypnotize me."

"When?"

"As soon as possible."

"I want to be there when she does," he admitted, and she nodded.

"I was hoping you would come," she confirmed as her cell phone began to ring. Chaz retrieved it from the end table and handed it to her. "It's Shelby." She clicked on. "Hi, Shelby. What's up?"

"Valencia, are you sitting down?!" Shelby exploded, entering her house, combing through some papers.

"What's going on?" Vinny asked, sitting up.

"All the slots have been *completely* booked for your show!" She continued in laughter. "Isn't that *wonderful*?!"

"Yes, that's great," Vinny tried to share her manager's enthusiasm, but Shelby's excitement was much too high to match.

"And, not only that, but *four* of your pieces have already been sold and one of *Parker's*, just from the website!"

"Awesome!"

"Want me to tell you which ones?"

"Not tonight. We'll talk tomorrow."

"Okay, honey. I'll see you tomorrow," Shelby concluded.

When Vinny hung up, she dropped her cell phone on the coffee table and stared into space. "Anything wrong, honey?" Chaz asked, sitting up.

"Shelby said four of my pieces and one of Parker's have sold already, and all the slots for the show have been completely filled," she explained nonchalantly.

Smiling wide, he indicated, "That's great, sweetie! What's the problem?!"

"No problem. I just wish I could remember," she confessed with a few tears rolling down her face. "Shelby wanted to tell me the pieces that were already sold, but I wouldn't let her. I was afraid I wouldn't remember them."

"Oh, baby," he sympathized, pulling her in his arms. "In time you will remember *everything*. I promise." He wiped her tears gently with his fingers and planted a soft kiss on her lips. "I love you so much."

She sniffed and replied, "I love you too." She smiled sweetly at him. "It's funny but it seems that the only thing I remember about our life is the love I have for you."

He smiled and kissed her again. "I don't know if I remember it, or it resurfaced because you've been so great. All I do know is that I love you very much." She was happy to have her husband in her life. No matter what happened next, she felt she would be ready.

****

"Jackson, there's a ten-thousand-dollar withdrawal from our bank account. Did you make that withdrawal?" Tammie Carson charged into her husband, as he entered the house. She was wearing rose-colored, soft-cotton pajamas and her shoulder-length, brown hair was flowing loosely in a silky wrap.

He focused on his excited wife and responded, "Honey, may I get into the house first before you start accusing me of something."

"This is *ten thousand dollars*, Jackson!" she countered.

"That was the money I donated to the children's ward at the hospital. Remember?" He lied, knowing that he couldn't tell her that he really withdrew the money to buy Shelby a diamond necklace for her birthday.

"Why did you withdraw the money instead of just writing a check?"

"I bought a cashier's check, honey."

"That doesn't make sense."

"What doesn't?" he snapped. "That I can't make decisions on my own?"

"I didn't say that, but..."

"No buts!" he ordered. "Now put that down and let the accountants take care of it."

"Jackson..."

"I'm going to bed," he announced then walked away quickly. "Good night." As he strolled up the staircase, he knew he had to be careful with Shelby. He cared a lot for her, but he couldn't let his affair with her jeopardize his marriage. He had plans to run for governor and maybe even senator, so he had to at least *pretend* to have a good marriage.

Tammie knew her husband was lying but why? She had put up with a few affairs in the past, but she would *not* do that again. He'd better hope that she didn't find out he was cheating again. She had *nothing* to keep her there now that their children are grown. She thought that maybe it was time to hire a private detective…and *soon*.

Chapter 9

The modestly decorated office was dimly lit with Chaz, in khaki pants and a navy-blue, button-down shirt, positioned on a sofa in the back, while Vinny, in tan capris and a button-down cashmere brown blouse, sat in her normal chair with Dr. Bruce, in her characteristic tailor-made, sky-blue skirt suit, sitting beside her. "Vinny, please close your eyes." Dr. Bruce instructed and she obeyed. "From here on, just nod your head instead of speaking. Do you understand?" Vinny nodded. "Are you comfortable?" She nodded again. "Good. Let's get started."

****

"Hi, honey," a petite, very thin, five-foot-six-inch, caramel-tanned young woman in a short, black, flare skirt with frills on the bottom, walked into the back room where Parker sat on a stool, painting in blue jeans, white T-shirt, blue denim baseball cap turned backward, and a blue painter's smock. Her shoulder-length smooth black hair was accented with dyed blonde streaks, causing a glow to her thin, oval face, highlighting her exotic, high cheekbones, and chiseled, jawline features.

"Hi, baby," he cooed, smiling, as she hugged him from the rear.

"How's it going?"

"Pretty well," he replied. "Sabrina, let me clean up before I get paint on you, baby." She backed away from him a little as he stood. "No practice today?"

"I'm finished for today. Where's Vinny?"

"She hasn't come in yet." he answered, washing his hands in the sink.

"Is she remembering anything yet?"

"Not yet."

"That must feel *crazy*!"

"Yeah. She's pretty upset about it," he acknowledged, grabbing her around her tiny waist and kissing her deeply. "How's my baby?"

"Healthy as a horse," she grinned, pushing her long, wavy hair out of her face.

"Let's see about that," he purred, pulling up her short skirt and sliding his hands in her panties, seizing her small butt. She moaned aloud as their lips caressed passionately. He dropped on the stool, pulling her on him, spreading her legs across his lap.

"When is Vinny coming in?" she cooed in his ear.

"Not for a while, I hope," he responded, unfastening her bra.

"Okay, you two, get a room," Shelby joked, while Sabrina laughed, and Parker refastened her bra.

"What're you doing here, Shelby?" He huffed as Sabrina stood. He had to reposition his excited body before he could stand.

"Obviously, interrupting something *important*," Shelby laughed.

"That's for damn sure!" he agreed, finally able to stand.

"Hi, Shelby," Sabrina snickered, punching Parker's arm.

"Hi, Sabrina. You might want to lock the front door when you want to *play* house," Shelby smirked.

"Nobody comes back here. They usually *stay* up front," he countered sarcastically.

"So, when is Valencia hiring another receptionist? Carmen has been gone for over six months."

"*Hello*...the boss has *amnesia*!" he sarcastically replied.

"Carmen got married and moved away long before Valencia's accident, *smartie*," she sarcastically retaliated.

"She was in the process of interviewing people before her accident, but it takes time to hire someone great," he explained. "You can't replace someone like Carmen too easily."

Changing the subject, Shelby inquired, "*Anyway*....where's my girl?"

"Don't know," Parker nonchalantly responded, very annoyed with her, standing there in that short, body-tight dress as old as she was. He had to admit that she was well preserved for a woman in her late forties.

Shelby added, "Did she tell you the good news?"

"I haven't talked to Vinny today," Parker confirmed. "What news?"

"*All* the slots are filled for the show."

"That's great," he acknowledged.

"There's more," Shelby beamed. "*Four* of Valencia's pieces have already been sold and *one* of *yours*."

"You're kidding!" he exploded.

"I kid you not!" Shelby shared his excitement.

"Honey, that's great!" Sabrina shrieked, jumping to him, and hugging him tight.

"Thanks, Shelby," he acknowledged. "That *is* good news."

Turning to leave, Shelby finalized, "Tell Valencia I'll talk to her later."

"Will do," Parker agreed, not being able to wipe the smile off his handsome face.

When Shelby was gone, Sabrina turned to Parker and suggested, "I better go, so you can continue your work, baby."

Grabbing her hand and swishing her in his arms, he blasted, "I know you're kidding!" She sniggered, and he planted a kiss on her lips. "Let me lock that damn door this time."

****

"How did I do?" Vinny wanted to know immediately.

"Very well," Dr. Bruce returned.

"How do you feel, baby?" Chaz inquired.

"I feel fine," she shared. "What did I say? Did you learn anything?"

"Do you have any new memories, Vinny?" probed Dr. Bruce.

"Not really. I remember there were a group of people there when that boy was shot. One of them seemed familiar, but I can't put my finger on it," she described. "What did I say?"

****

"*Hypnosis*?! Are you freaking kidding me?!"

"That don't mean she gonna remember anything," Frankie insisted on his cell phone, sitting on the yard swing.

"Frankie, she's going to remember. It's *just* a matter of time. Kenneth's body was found and identified, and they have been flashing his picture all over the media. If she remembers, we are all screwed," the person with the snake, pinky ring demanded. "No more playing around. She has *got* to go! Make up your mind. Are you *in*... or *out*?!"

****

"You're still blocking out some things, Vinny," Dr. Bruce shared. "It seems like you saw the killers, but you're blocking out their faces. We can try it again later."

"Next session?" she posed as Chaz took her hand.

"No, not the next session. I want to give your senses time to relax," the doctor rationalized.

"So, you didn't learn anything new?" Vinny bade.

Dr. Bruce handed her a piece of paper and shared, "I had you draw the picture of the murdered man. You drew this." Vinny studied the picture carefully. "This young man's body was just found. Did you know him?" Vinny shook her head.

"I saw him in one of my flashbacks."

"Did you report it to the police?"

Chaz added, "There was nothing to report. She didn't see the perpetrators, and I was afraid the police would put her through unnecessary stress, trying to force her to remember, or worse, trying to pin it on her."

"I see what you mean," the doctor agreed. "Maybe it would be better to hold off on reporting it to the police until we have more information." Dr. Bruce paused. "What about the almost hit-and-run? Did the police find that person?" Vinny shook her head. "I don't want to alarm you, but maybe you *should* consider involving the police after what happened. The police might be able to provide protection for you. It sounds like somebody is getting extremely nervous about you regaining your memory. You might be in *real* danger." Dr. Bruce focused on Chaz. "*Both* of you."

****

"You're a *bad* girl, Miss Sabrina Charles," Parker teased as they kissed at the front door of the studio, with him towering over her small frame.

"But you *love* me," she teased back, kissing him again.

"I most certainly do," he cooed, and they kissed again. "Coming over tonight?"

"Of course," she agreed, as the door opened, almost hitting them, and Vinny walked through it slowly.

"Oh, sorry, you two. Did I hit you?" she asked.

"No, you're good," he responded.

"How are you?" Vinny added, directing her question to the girl she didn't recognize.

"Hi, Vinny," Sabrina greeted.

"Vinny, this is Sabrina Charles, my girlfriend," Parker introduced.

"Hi, Sabrina," she greeted. "You are a pretty girl."

"Thank you," Sabrina accepted.

"So, you're the dancer?" Vinny acknowledged.

"Yes. How did you know?" Sabrina inquired, then focused on Parker. "Oh, I forgot. You told her." He nodded as Vinny walked to the counter, and then Sabrina turned to Parker. "See you later."

"Can't wait," he replied, then kissed her again.

"Bye, Vinny," she called as she left.

"Bye, Sabrina," she answered back, pulling on a painter's smock. "Did Shelby come by today?"

"Yeah. She told me the good news," he admitted.

"That *is* good news, isn't it!" she shared his enthusiasm.

"Yeah, I'll say."

"Sabrina seems nice."

"She is. Thank you."

"Is she the *one*?"

"Yeah. I think so," he acknowledged a little blushed, following her into the back room.

"Then why haven't you married her?"

"We're trying to get our careers off the ground first. I don't want to get married and struggle financially."

"That's smart," she agreed, sitting on her stool at her canvas to finish a painting. "Do we have any more of that glowing red?"

"Yeah. I'll get it."

"Thank you, Parker. I don't know what I'm going to do without you."

"Where I'm going?" he chuckled, putting the paint on the table beside her easel.

"You're going to have your own career."

"Oh, that's a ways yet."

"I don't think so."

"Well, I hope I could stay here with you, even if my paintings do start selling well."

"Really?"

"Yeah. I like working for you."

"That's so sweet," she cooed as the doorbell rang. "Who can that be?"

"I'll get it," he offered.

Thinking of the hit-and-run attempt, she stated, "I'd better go with you."

When Vinny and Parker stepped into the front, they witnessed two people wearing ski masks through the glass windows. Suddenly, they whipped out AR 15 rifles and opened fire through the glass.

****

"What is it, Chaz?" Monica questioned, entering his office with a low-cut, silk blouse and a dress so short, it barely covered her round behind. The belt around her waist and the six-inch heels caused the dress to be accented even more seductively, hacking it up in the back.

"Sit please, Monica," he advised as he sat behind his desk.

"What's up?" she queried, sitting in front of his desk, and crossing her legs, exposing almost all of her thick thighs.

"Monica, I intended to talk to you Friday, but you weren't here," he cautiously started. "I really need to talk to you about the dress code here."

"Why? Is someone complaining about how I dress?" she retorted, and he could tell that she was getting upset.

"Take it easy, Monica."

"I bet it was that nosy Brooke Myers! Her ass is too old to dress cute, so she doesn't want me to!" she snapped, jumping up.

"That's not it. Monica," he defended, rising from his chair also. "Please calm down." He handed her a small pamphlet.

"What's this?"

"The staff handbook. Please read the section on the dress code for staff members."

"But it's almost *summer*!"

"The dress code is *always* in effect because we have parents, district staff, board members, etc. coming in here all the time," he explained. "I do allow everyone to dress casually during the summer months but keeping in mind the dress code."

"So, you're taking that bitch's side?!"

"I'm on the side of the *rules*. You know that!"

"Chaz, I..." she started but was interrupted by Chaz' ringing office phone.

"Excuse me," he offered, picking up his phone. "Dr. Perkins." Paused. "*What*?!" He yelled. "Are they all right?!"

Chapter 10

"Mrs. Perkins, how do you feel?" The police detective questioned Vinny as they sat in the hospital lounge.

"I'm okay. How is Parker?"

"He's in surgery," the detective shared as Chaz burst through the door, and Vinny stood to meet him.

"Honey, what happened?" He exploded as he hugged her tightly, and she burst into tears.

"It happened so fast," she cried. "Parker got shot trying to protect me."

"Mr. Perkins?" the detective asked, and he nodded. "I'm Detective Jerry Harper." He extended a hand, Chaz took it, and they ended in a firm handshake. Detective Harper was a forty-eight-year-old, medium-built Caucasian man, a little taller than Chaz, wearing a cheap, dark-gray suit. His brown hair was cut short and combed to the back to hide a bald spot at the top.

"Hello, Detective?" He accepted. "Chaz Perkins." He focused on his wife. "Sit down, sweetie." She obeyed, and he sat beside her on the couch, while Detective Harper sat in a chair opposite them. "What happened, honey?"

Vinny took a deep breath, wiped her tears with the Kleenex from the table and began, "Parker and I heard the doorbell. When we started for the door, they started shooting, and Parker shielded me from the bullets by knocking me to the floor. When the alarm sounded, they ran, and then I noticed that Parker had been shot." She stopped when the doctor entered and rushed to him. "How is Parker?"

"We removed two bullets, one from his leg and one from his stomach. Luckily, no major organs were hit," the doctor explained.

"Is he going to be all right?" Vinny wanted to know.

"Yes, he'll be fine. They'll be bringing him into a room soon. Room 323," the doctor shared.

"Thank you, Doctor," she acknowledged.

"You're welcome," the doctor finalized, walking away.

"Thank God," Vinny breathed. "My God, I don't know how to get in touch with his parents or his girlfriend."

"Shelby probably can help you with that," Chaz suggested.

"Oh yeah," agreed Vinny.

"Mrs. Perkins, I still need to ask you some more questions," Detective Harper reminded.

"Sure," she agreed, sitting again, followed by Chaz and the Detective. "What do you need to know?"

"Do you know of anyone who would want to hurt either you or Mr. Grayson?"

"It's *me*," she admitted. "I was in a car accident a couple months ago. I was in a coma for six weeks. I can't remember my life."

"What're you mean, you can't *remember* your life?"

She took a breath then shared, "I have amnesia, Detective."

"*Total* amnesia?"

"Yes, I don't remember any portion of my life before the accident. I don't even remember my name, my wedding, my parents, or *anything*," she explained. "All I know is what everyone has told me since I came out of the coma."

"So, why do you think someone is trying to hurt you?"

"Because someone tried to run me down last week," she explained, as Chaz took her hand.

"Did you report it?"

"Of course, I did."

"Do you know who investigated?"

"Several officers showed up at the studio. I don't know their names."

"Was Mr. Grayson with you then too?"

"Yes, he's the one who saved me."

"If Mr. Grayson was with you both times, I still don't understand why you are so sure that the perpetrator was after *you* instead of *him*."

Vinny took a deep breath then confessed, "Because I experienced a flashback a couple of times, and I think I witnessed a… *murder*."

****

Sabrina, in a short nightshirt, paced around in Parker's apartment, wondering where he was. He wasn't answering his cell phone. She observed eight-thirty on the clock then sat in front of the television set. Suddenly, her cell phone sounded, and she picked it up quickly. "Hello?"

"Sabrina, this is Shelby," she announced, sitting in the studio with her husband as men repaired the glass windows.

"Hi, Shelby."

"Honey, listen. Something happened at the studio today. Vinny didn't know how to get in touch with you. I had to come to the studio to look in the cabinet for your number in Parker's files," she explained.

"What's wrong, Shelby?" Sabrina inquired. "Did something else happen?"

"Yes. Parker is in the hospital."

"*Hospital*! What happened?" she shrieked.

"He'll be fine, but he was shot."

"*Shot*?!"

****

"What do you mean, you *think* you witnessed a murder?" Detective Harper asked with his face growing red.

"It was in my flashback. I think it was the boy that was just found, Kenneth Lewis."

"Did you tell this to the policemen who investigated the hit-and-run attempt?"

"No, I didn't know it was Kenneth Lewis until later."

"You should've reported this new flashback as soon as you knew it was Kenneth Lewis, Mrs. Perkins," Detective Harper insisted. "You could be our only lead to his murder."

"But I don't know anything," she stressed. "I just saw him falling and that's it."

"But *someone* thinks you can identify him," the detective hypothesized.

"But I can't."

"But *they* think you can, or they wouldn't be trying to *kill* you."

Chapter 11

Parker opened his eyes slowly, and Sabrina leaped from the chair beside his hospital bed. "Hi, honey. How do you feel?"

"Like I've been hit by a Mack truck," he squeezed out.

Sabrina smiled and picked up his hand. "Do you remember what happened?"

"Yes, two guys shot up the studio," he replied, as the nurse entered. "How is Vinny?"

"She's fine. She didn't get shot," she shared.

"Hi, Parker," the nurse singsong, smiling wide. "I'm Ashley. I will be your nurse today. How are you doing?" Nurse Ashley couldn't help but notice how handsome Parker was and wondered if his relationship with this skinny girl was serious.

"You tell me," he joked.

"Do you remember what happened?" she asked, and he nodded. "Well, you were hit with two bullets, one in your right thigh and one on the left side of your stomach. The good thing is that no major organs were hit, so you're going to be just fine. You'll be a little sore for a while, and we'll measure you for some crutches to help you get around. Do you have any questions?"

"No, not right now."

"I'll be right back to take your vitals," Nurse Ashley said, bouncing out, with her long, blonde ponytail swinging from side to side.

Sabrina resented the pretty nurse immediately. She was *too* friendly and *too* pretty. She noticed how Nurse Ashley looked at Parker, and she didn't like it. She knew she couldn't leave her man alone, vulnerable to this Nurse Ashley all day. She turned her attention back to Parker and announced, "I called your parents. They couldn't get a flight out today, but they will be here tomorrow."

"They don't have to come. I'm fine," he recognized, sitting up in bed.

"Well, your mother was very upset."

"Mom is like that," he acknowledged, as Ashley reentered with a water bottle full of ice and water.

"I brought you some water," she expressed in her own perky way.

"Thank you," he observed.

She placed the bottle on his tray then pushed it beside his bed. She proceeded to fluff his pillow behind his back to help him sit up better. "I'll be back in a few minutes," she shared, and he nodded. "Can I get you anything else?" She thought, *A good lay?*

"No," he rejected. "I'm okay."

You are more than okay, handsome, she thought then patted his hand and added, "See you soon." He nodded, and she winked at him before she left.

"Oh, no she didn't!" Sabrina yelped.

"What?"

"You know what! That cunt was flirting with you!"

"She was just being nice."

"She was *flirting*!" she insisted. "I swear, Parker, you wouldn't know a flirt if it hit you in the face!"

"Calm down."

"I'm gonna report her ass!"

"Report what…that she *winked*?" he replied sarcastically. "Ooh, she ought to be horse whipped." He laughed, and she had to laugh with him.

She chortled, "That *skank*!"

****

"Brooke, why did you go to *Chaz* about the way I dress instead of coming to *me*?" Monica charged, bursting through Brooke's opened office door. "I thought we were cool."

"I wanted to talk to you, but Chaz said he would do it." Brooke retaliated. "And we *are* cool."

"So, it *was* you," Monica confirmed. "Chaz wouldn't tell me who complained. I knew it wasn't Bobby or Chase."

Brooke smiled slightly and remarked with a little sarcasm, "No, *they* wouldn't."

"Is this okay, Madam *Warden*?" she sarcastically asked, indicating her dress, which was just above her knees.

"You look fine," Brooke acknowledged.

"Thanks," she spat sarcastically, turning to leave.

"Monica," the AP called. "I hope this won't cause any tension between us. You are a good worker, and I like working with you. And when Chaz isn't here, I'm in charge."

"Brooke, let's get something straight," the angry young woman clarified. "I don't like you. I think you are an opportunist, and Chaz had better watch his back. So, you stay outta my way, and I'll stay outta yours."

"I'm sorry you feel that way," she recognized. "I thought we got along fine."

"I do my job. That doesn't mean I gotta like you."

"Since we're being honest, I suggest you leave Chaz alone. He's a happily married man."

Monica just stared at Brooke for a moment, and then she came back with, "Chaz is a big boy. He can take care of himself. He doesn't need some nosy ass, over-the-hill *bitty* trying to run his life! As I said, stay the hell away from me…or you'll be sorry!"

"Is that a threat?"

The young woman stopped, turned around to face the older woman head-on and snapped, "*Yes!*"

****

Vinny was awakened by Chaz bathing her face and neck with soft, sweet kisses. She smiled and he pressed his lips on hers. "Good morning," he cooed.

"Good morning," she whispered, and he kissed her again. "Can I brush my teeth?"

"You're sweet enough," he replied, gently pulling her in his arms.

"Aren't you late for work, Doc?" she teased as she stroked his hairy chest gently with her fingers.

"I took off. I want to be with you today."

"Is the policeman still outside?"

"Yes, he's still there. Detective Harper said you'll have around the clock protection until either they figure out what's going on or you remember who killed Kenneth Lewis."

"Baby, I need to go to the hospital to check on Parker and then to the studio to work. My show is next month."

"That's fine, darling. I'll go with you," he made known. "I'm not letting you out of my sight today."

****

"What?!" Mrs. Dow screamed, and Frankie ran into the kitchen, followed by Justine, to see what happened.

"Mom, what's wrong?" her daughter inquired.

"I just saw on the news that there was a shooting at Vinny's studio yesterday."

"What?!" Justine shrieked. "Is she alright?"

"Yes. Parker was shot twice, but he's going to be all right?"

"What about Vinny?" Frankie asked. "Is she alright?"

"Yes. She wasn't shot. Parker somehow saved her."

"Oh my God!" Justine squawked. "What is this world coming to? So, Parker *is* all right?"

"The news said he's okay," their mother replied, and Frankie dropped his head. He hated that he couldn't share anything with anybody because he was just as much involved with Kenneth's murder as anyone else. He also knew that they would keep on coming after his sister…until they *killed* her.

****

"Good morning," Vinny greeted, entering Parker's hospital room with her husband, and a policeman waiting outside the door. Vinny placed a bouquet of flowers on the table.

"Hi, Vinny, Chaz," Parker responded, adjusting his bed to a seated position.

"Hi, Sabrina," Vinny spoke.

"Hello," Sabrina responded.

"Hi, Sabrina," added Chaz.

"Hi, Chaz," she acknowledged.

"How are you, Parker?" Vinny wanted to know.

"I'm okay," he answered.

Vinny sniffed back tears and announced, "It's my fault, Parker. I'm so sorry."

"No, it's not *your* fault," he insisted. "It's the scumbags that shot me."

"But they were after *me*." she added.

"You don't know that," Parker demanded. "And even if they were after you, it's still not *your* fault, so I don't wanna hear that!"

"Parker, thank you so much for looking after Vinny," Chaz offered.

"I have to protect her. Without her I don't have a job," he joked.

Vinny smiled with him then sobered quickly. "Do you know when you're going home?"

"In a couple days," he revealed.

"Sabrina, have you been here all night?" Vinny asked.

"Yeah, I couldn't leave my baby," she cooed, touching his hand.

"Why don't you take a break. Go home and get a few hours of sleep," Vinny suggested. "We'll be here."

"Yes, honey. Go and get some rest," Parker agreed. "I know you didn't get any sleep last night. The nurses woke us up every hour to take my vitals."

"Are you sure you don't mind staying?" Sabrina asked.

"Not at all," confirmed Vinny.

"All right," she agreed. "I won't be long."

"Take your time," Vinny suggested.

"Thank you," she accepted then kissed Parker before leaving.

"Vinny, how are *you* doing?" Parker inquired. "You must be so scared."

"I am a little concerned, but I'm fine. Thanks to you," she acknowledged, as her cell phone began to ring. "It's Detective Harper. Hello?"

"Mrs. Perkins?" the detective said on the other end of the telephone, sitting at his desk in the busy police station.

"Yes. Hello, Detective."

"Good news. We have identified the two men who attacked you and Mr. Grayson. We'll sending a car to pick them up just as soon as we get the warrant."

"Really?!" Vinny screamed then focused on Chaz and Parker. "They know who attacked us."

"Great!" Chaz exploded.

"Wonderful!" added Parker.

"Mrs. Perkins," Detective Harper called. "We're going to find out why they did it and if someone hired them, which more than likely, someone did, I'll let you know what we find out."

"Thank you, Detective."

"You're welcome," he accepted. "You'll still have protection until further notice."

"Thank you," she responded then hung up. "Isn't that great?"

"It sure is, baby," Chaz agreed.

"Did he give you their names?" asked Parker.

"No. They're picking them up as soon as they get a warrant. He said he would find out why they attacked us and will get back in touch with us," she explained.

"That's great, honey," Chaz chimed in.

"It sure is," added Parker.

"Parker, where're your parents?" Vinny asked.

"They live in Chicago," he answered. "Sabrina called them, and they'll be here today."

"I look forward to meeting them," Vinny concurred, as the door opened and an attractive pecan-tanned, tall lady with short, curly, black hair and a tall Caucasian man with brown, wavy hair walked in, looking very distinguished, casually dressed in slacks and shirts.

The lady rushed to Parker's bed and pulled him in her arms as tears flowed down her face. "I'm all right, Mom," he shared.

The man extended a hand to Chaz and introduced, "Hi, I'm August Grayson."

Taking his hand in a shake, Chaz accepted, "Hello, Mr. Grayson. I'm Chaz Perkins and this is my wife, Vinny."

"Hello," he acknowledged, extending a hand to Vinny. "I've heard so much about you. It's a pleasure to finally meet you."

Shaking his hand, Vinny recognized, "Likewise, Mr. Grayson. Thank you."

Parker's mother finally released him, wiped her eyes, and focused on Vinny and Chaz. "I'm sorry," she apologized. "I'm Marilyn Grayson."

"Nice to meet you," Chaz accepted, and Vinny just smiled with a slight nod.

"Well, we'll leave you all alone so you can visit," Vinny suggested then touched Parker's hand. "We'll be back soon." He nodded. Chaz and Vinny left, extending farewells to the Graysons as they left.

Mrs. Grayson focused on her son and demanded, "Parker, if working for her is putting you in danger, you need to quit...*immediately*!"

****

"How in the hell could they miss?!" the person with the snake pinky ring yelled on the telephone. "I'm dealing with fucking idiots!" Pause. "The cops have already identified those bumbling fools. You clean this mess up!" the person raged. "I am not sticking around until that bitch fingers me and put a noose around my neck! I want that bitch dead...*now*!"

****

Ryan opened the door in gray pajamas that reached just below his knees with a matching button-down, short-sleeve pajama shirt, and Justine was standing there smiling wide in red Daisy Dukes and a red and white sleeveless tube top, exposing her belly button. "Hey, this is a pleasant surprise. What're you doing here?" he beamed, giving her a big kiss.

"Do I need a reason to visit my man?" she replied, moving past him and into the medium-size, ranch-style brick house.

"You know you don't" he stressed, kissing her again. "Want some breakfast? Mom just cooked."

"I already ate, but I will have some orange juice while *you* eat."

"Come on," he concurred, taking her hand, and leading her into the kitchen where his mother sat, with blue flowery-print scrubs on, and her hair in a neat, short ponytail.

"Good morning, Mrs. Henry," Justine addressed.

"Hi, Justine," the lady responded dryly. "What're you doing up and out so early?"

"I had to run some errands and decided to stop by."

"Would you like something to eat?"

"I'll just have some orange juice. I've already eaten. Thank you though," she accepted, pouring herself a glass of orange juice in the glass that Ryan handed to her.

"It's not that early, Mom," he defended. "It's almost eleven."

"Oh yeah. I almost forgot I'm on second shift this week," his mother acknowledged, smiling with crooked, cigarette-stained teeth. "How is your family, Justine?"

"Everybody's fine. Thank you for asking."

"How is school?" Mrs. Henry inquired again.

"Great. Thank you."

"And Vinny? Is she regaining her memory?" Mrs. Henry asked, wondering where in the world was this girl's clothes. She had two grown daughters, and there was no way she would've *ever* let them run around half-naked like that.

"Not yet," Justine shared, admiring this woman who had raised her three children alone after her husband died in a car crash while her children were still incredibly young. Ryan was the baby, and his two sisters didn't live in town anymore. One of them was a lawyer and the other one a teacher.

"Well, I gotta get going. We have three surgeries today." Mrs. Henry announced, getting up, still chewing on her last mouthful of food, and drinking the last sip of coffee. She planted a kiss on Ryan's forehead. "See ya, honey."

"Bye, Mom," he acknowledged, still chewing.

"Justine, have a good day, sweetheart," Mrs. Henry finalized, leaving.

"You too, Ma'am," Justine called back.

When Mrs. Henry was gone, Justine moved and straddled across Ryan's lap, and she felt his body immediately respond and she smiled. "Good morning," she cooed, and they kissed long and passionately.

"Good morning," he groaned, smiling wide.

"I thought your mother was already at work," she laughed.

"I never know what time my mother is leaving," he joined her laughter, kissing her again, then bathing her neck with kisses. "Um, you smell good."

"So do you. You smell like *bacon*," she chuckled then burst into laughter.

He laughed with her as he buried his face in her chest, taking in the aroma of her fresh scent.

****

"Police!" Several police officers burst into a hotel room with weapons drawn. The room was dingy and dark with a foul odor that caused the officers to gasp for fresh air. Everything seemed to be in order, except for a few clothes thrown on the floor and on the two unmade beds.

The officers frantically but cautiously searched the room until they stumbled across one body in the bathtub, full of bloody water, and the other body behind the bed, resting in a pool of blood.

"*Damn*!" Detective Harper spat. "We're too late!"

****

Vinny sat in Parker's hospital room, watching the news on television with him. Chaz had gone to work for a while, Sabrina hadn't returned to the hospital yet, and his parents went to his apartment to freshen up. "Mayor Carson, what're you doing about the crime here? It's getting out of control," the news reporter asked.

The tall, distinguish looking African American man focused on the reporter and announced, "We have assigned five percent more police officers on duty at all times, we have place ten percent more streetlights on almost every street, and we have begun holding neighborhood watch meetings in various communities. We are taking every precaution to protect our citizens."

"Mayor Carson is the best thing this city has ever had," Parker stated his opinion.

"Is he? I can't remember," Vinny inquired.

"Yeah, He's a home-grown boy."

"Impressive."

"What's more impressive is that he came from a single parent home and grew up in the projects. He earned scholarships to college and law school. He's truly a great American story," Parker explained. "Mayor Carson cleaned up many of the drug-infested areas. His life has been threatened so many times, but he keeps going. My hero!"

"Mayor Carson, what about the attempts on Valencia Perkins' life," the reporter was asking.

"That's *me*!" Vinny shrieked. "I'm on *tv*!"

"You're famous, sweetheart," Parker laughed with her.

"Mrs. Perkins has been assigned twenty-four-hour police protection until we sort this out," Mayor Carson replied.

Vinny turned to Parker. "The *mayor* knows me?"

"Yes, he's one of your biggest supporters. He has several of your paintings in his house," he confirmed.

"I'm flattered," she beamed as Sabrina entered.

"Hi," she greeted, planting a kiss on Parker's lips. "I'm sorry I'm so late getting back. I fell asleep."

"No problem, baby," he responded. "I wanted you to get some sleep."

"Are your parents here yet?"

"Yes. I told them to go to my apartment to get some rest. They came here straight from the airport," he explained.

"That's good," she acknowledged. "Vinny, thank you for staying."

"No problem. We're fine."

"Cause I gotta guard him. These little nurses are trying to test my patience, especially that little blonde-headed slut named Ashley," Sabrina spat.

"You're a trip!" Parker laughed.

Laughing also, Vinny added, "I'll help you fight them off."

"Don't encourage her. *Please*!" He yelped, and Sabrina kissed him again. "Well, you don't have to worry about that. I'm going home in the morning."

"That's great, sweetheart," Sabrina cheered as Detective Harper entered with a long face, and Vinny noticed right away.

She asked cautiously, "What's wrong?"

****

"Hey, Lance, your daughter on the news!" a man yelled, as a roomful of men in orange jumpsuits, worked in the kitchen at the prison.

"Who?" a medium-height, very dark man with a straggly beard asked.

"The artist," another man replied. "Ain't she your girl?"

"That's what her mama say," Lance Greene nonchalantly replied, washing dishes.

Bursting into laughter, another man replied, "What'd you mean, that's what her *mama* say? She *is* your girl, ain't she?"

"Mommy's *baby*, daddy's *maybe*," Lance commented, rubbing his kinky, brushy hair.

"Do she ever come to see you?" another man with missing front teeth asked.

"She's too high and mighty to come here!" Lance snarled.

"Man, give the girl some credit!" the first man joined in again. "Before she went loony, she used to visit you all the time."

"She sure is pretty," the toothless man added.

"Then she can't be Greene girl!" another man laughed.

Lance Greene stopped washing dishes, focused on the men, and finalized, "She's *not*."

"If she ain't your girl, then who her daddy?" Mr. Toothless wanted to know.

Lance stretched his blood-shot eyes, tilted his head to one side and concluded, "The hell if I know!"

****

"Good evening, Detective," Vinny welcomed Detective Harper at her door. "Please come in."

"Hello, Mrs. Perkins," he responded, coming in as Chaz was entering the foyer also.

"Hi, Detective," Chaz spoke, shaking the man's hand. "How are you?"

"I'm okay," Detective Harper returned.

"Come in, Detective," offered Vinny.

"Thank you," he replied, following her into the den as Chaz trailed behind.

"Please have a seat," Chaz offered, and Detective Harper sat in a chair while Chaz and Vinny shared the couch. "Do you have anything new?"

"Mrs. Perkins, we have no doubt that your life is in danger. Whatever you saw before you lost your memory, someone doesn't want you to remember it," the detective explained. "I have the Mayor, the Chief of Police, the media, everyone on me to solve this case." He focused on Vinny. "It seems that you have a lot of fans, Mrs. Perkins." She acknowledged his compliment with a sweet smile.

"So, what's next, Detective?" Chaz wanted to know, taking his wife's hand.

"I'll be your house guest during the night for the next few weeks, until we catch this guy," he explained.

"We will still have a man stationed outside at all times for your protection."

"Is all this necessary?" Vinny wanted to know.

"Mrs. Perkins, I don't want to scare you, but the men who attacked you and were then murdered themselves were street thugs, but the hit on them was *professional*," Detective Harper explained cautiously.

"What're you saying?" Chaz questioned. "There's a professional *hit* on my wife?!"

Chapter 12

"Hi, Parker. How're you feeling? I didn't expect you to come to work so soon," Vinny spoke to her assistant as he hobbled on one crutch into the back room of the studio where she stood from her stool to welcome him. "It's only been a week."

"Hi, beautiful," he greeted, planting a kiss on her cheek.

"How're you doing?"

"I'm doing fine. Thank you," he acknowledged, sitting on a stool in front of his unfinished painting.

"Did your parents get off okay?"

"Yeah. I was glad to see them leave too."

She chuckled, "Why?"

"Cause my mom wants me to quit working for you until they find out who's trying to hurt you."

"That might not be a bad idea, Parker."

"Are you *kidding*?!" he shrieked. "I'm about to feature some pieces in your show. I'll take my chances."

"If you say so."

"I do," he finalized.

"How are you making it at home on those crutches?"

"I'm doing okay. Sabrina is staying with me to help."

"Sabrina is very sweet."

"Yes, she is. I don't know what I would do without her," he acknowledged. "If she wasn't so jealous, she would be perfect."

"Well, she's young and in love. Be patient with her."

"I try, Vinny. I try," he chuckled. "So, I see we have firepower."

"Yes, we do," she acknowledged. "Parker, I'm serious about you quitting for a while. The police think there's a professional contract on me. If you don't feel safe here, you could always work at home."

"With all this protection!" he joked. "I'm safer here than home."

"I just don't want you to get hurt again."

****

"Your sister is being guarded twenty-four-seven," the person with the snake pinky ring said over the telephone to Frankie.

"I hear you put out a contract on her." Frankie inquired on his cell phone, while he sat outside on the tree swing.

"I had to do *something*. These amateurs weren't getting results."

"I told you; you didn't have to do *anything*. She don't remember *nothing*," Frankie insisted.

"Well, I'm not waiting around until she does!"

"We have a shipment coming on Friday."

"Don't worry about that right now. I have another job for you."

"What is it?"

"We might need you to do your sister."

"What?!" Frankie exploded. "You want me to *kill* my own *sister*?!"

"She's being guarded around the clock," the person stated. "*We* can't get to her, but *you* can, and we need it done *soon*!"

****

"About seventy-five percent of our eLearning students are working consistently, so we need to reach out to the ones who aren't working, to see what the problem is," Brooke explained, sitting with Chaz in his office.

"Yes, I talked to the other two high school principals, and they are having problems with face-to-face attendance," he explained. "I hope this hybrid model we are piloting this year is successful. I like the idea of students having choices."

"I do too. High school students are almost adults; they *need* choices," she agreed. "We…" Monica entered, cutting her off.

"Chaz, there is a parent up front, ranting and raving," she blurted out.

"Is Robin up there?" he asked, standing.

"Yes, she is, but she can't calm the lady down."

"Why didn't she call me?" he asked, rushing out, followed by Brooke and Monica.

"I don't know," replied Monica. "You know Robin. She thinks she can handle *anything*."

When Chaz, Brooke and Monica entered the visitor's booth, the parent was yelling, "I'm trying to tell you! How can Jeremy do work on the Chromebook when we don't have Internet?! I am a single mom with *four* children! I can't afford Internet! And Jeremy helps take care of his sisters and brother when I'm at work, so he can't come to school every day! That's why I signed him up for eLearning!"

"Miss Jones," Chaz interrupted, and she jerked around and focused on him.

"Dr. Perkins, I'm trying to tell this woman…" she raged as Robin, the receptionist, an albino woman with bright red hair looked on.

"It's okay. I understand," he tried to soothe the upset mother. "Let's go into the conference room, so I can understand your issues, please." She glared at him for a moment then nodded. "Brooke, come with me, please."

"Sure."

Chaz, Brooke, and Miss Jones walked into the conference room and sat at the large table. "Miss Jones, you know Mrs. Myers, correct?"

"Yes," the lady replied. "Hi."

"Hello, Miss. Jones."

"What seems to be the problem, Miss Jones?" he asked.

"Dr. Perkins, I tried to get Internet for my house, but every company I checked with said it would be over sixty dollars a month. I can't afford that. I'm working two jobs now just to put food on the table," the lady explained.

Focusing on Brooke, Chaz inquired, "Don't we have some extra hot spots available?"

"I don't know," she answered. "We could check with Chase."

Chaz retrieved his radio transmitter from his hip and called, "One to four."

"Go ahead one," a voice replied.

"Would you please come to the main conference room?"

"In route," he acknowledged. "Ten-four."

Focusing back on the mother, Chad explained, "Miss Jones, I think we can help you. We ordered some hot spots for our students to use in the classrooms where the wi-fi is unstable. I'm sure we could allow you to borrow one for your children to use at home."

"That would be great, Dr. Perkins," Miss Jones said, smiling for the first time, as a short, young African American, milk-chocolate-tanned man with short twists in her hair entered, wearing a black track suit.

"Hello, everyone," he spoke, and they returned his greeting.

"Miss Jones, do you know Mr. Taylor?" Chaz asked and she nodded, then he focused back on the young man. "Chase, do we have any of those hot spots available that Miss Jones could take home for her children to be able to use the Internet?"

"Yes, Sir," Chase replied. "I'll go and get one."

"Great," Chaz recognized. "Please take Miss Jones with you, so she can check one out."

"Sure," the young man agreed, and Miss Jones stood with him.

"Thank you so much, Dr. Perkins," she said, smiling wide.

"You're very welcome," he accepted. "I'm glad we could help."

"This way," Chase escorted her out.

"Good job, boss," Brooke complemented Chaz, as Monica frowned at them through the small glass in the conference room door.

****

Shelby went clacking in the back of the studio in her six-inch, black pumps, wine-color, knee-length, flare dress, and flawless jewelry. "Valencia! Parker!" she shrieked in her high-pitched voice. "What're y'all trying to do to me? Getting shot, run down, and hospitalized! Are you two all right?!"

Vinny and Parker shared a smile. They were always amused at Shelby's energy. "Hi, Shell," Parker singsong.

"Parker, you dear boy," Shelby cooed, pinching his cheeks. "Are you two going to be ready by July?"

"Of course," assured Vinny. "Right, Parker?"

"Um hummm," he singsong again.

"You know that's next month, right?"

"We know, Shelby," Vinny acknowledged.

"Good, cause the Governor is coming, the mayor is coming, local and federal judges are coming, art critics are coming. We're gonna have a full house," Shelby raved.

"I thought we were making appointments," Vinny checked.

"We are, and all the slots have been filled. Don't worry. I'll take care of everything!" Shelby chuckled. "Y'all just *stay alive!*" She burst into laughter.

"Not funny, Shelby," Parker responded, and Vinny just shook her head.

****

"I see that the wicked witch of the west is all up in your face," Monica snapped, entering Chad's office.

"What?" he asked, looking up from his computer.

"I see *Msssss Brooke* all in your face," she repeated.

He chuckled, "What're you talking about?"

"She already has *one* brutha. I guess she wants *another* one," she commented, sitting in front of his desk.

Chaz turned and focused on Monica for the first time and shared, "I wish you and Brooke would get along. We all have to work together, and it would make all our jobs easier if you did."

"I don't need to get along with her," she insisted.

"*Yes*, you do," he stressed. "We are all here for the students. They come first."

"Then she should mind her own business!"

"The school *is* her business, Monica," he stressed. "You're part of the school, so as long as you're *at* the school, you're *her* business too."

"Are you *defending* her?"

"Yes, because she happens to be right," he held his ground, and she just stared at him. "It's not *personal*. It's *business*."

"But I've been dressing like this for years. Why is she *just* saying something?"

"Because the district office is getting on us about dress code violations, and we've had to crack down."

Brooke walked to Chaz's office door and was about to enter when she heard Monica's voice, so she froze at the door.

Monica's voice soften, as she cooed, "Don't you like the way I dress, Chaz?"

"That has nothing to do with it."

"But you do, don't you?" she singsong again, wanting to corner him into admitting that he was interested in her.

Chaz sensed what Monica was trying to do, and he didn't want to mislead her, so he politely replied, "Honestly, Monica, my *wife* is the *only* woman I notice in that way."

Brooke smiled wide, never having more respect for Chaz than at this very moment, then she knocked on the open door.

"Hello," she spoke politely, but Monica just ignored her and stormed out, and Brooke thought, *Set your sights on someone else's husband, Miss Thang! But be careful because there are still decent men out there!*

****

"Here, baby," a bronze color, biracial young lady said to Frankie, putting a lit cigarette in his mouth.

"Thanks, Darlene," Frankie accepted, sitting on one side of a booth in a dimly lit bar, while Jarrick and Muriel, a caramel-tanned lady with long, straight, blonde weaved hair, sat on the other side.

"Where are our drinks?" Jarrick snapped, looking back, just as a waitress brought over a tray with drinks. "It's about time, Linda. What took you so long?"

"I'm sorry, Jarrick. Debbie is running late," the waitress replied, distributing their drinks. "I'm working by myself."

"No problem, Linda," Frankie spoke up. "Jarrick is always impatient."

"Can I get y'all anything else?" The frazzled waitress asked.

"No. We're good," Frankie answered, and then she walked off.

"Muriel, there's a sale at the mall this weekend," Darlene shared. "Wanna go?"

"Sure," she agreed.

"Jarrick, wanna go to the sale at Walmart this weekend?" Frankie joked, trying to make his voice sound like the girls.

"Oh, yes," Jarrick played along, in his impression of a woman's voice. "Let's do that."

"Nut job!" Darlene laughed, shoving Frankie on the arm, while all of them laughed.

"Hey, Frankie, how is your sister?" Muriel asked.

"Does she really have *amnesia*?" added Darlene.

"Yeah, that's true," he confirmed.

"Is her show still on?" questioned Jarrick.

"How would I know?!" Frankie snapped. "I don't buy *art*." They burst into laughter as Frankie's cell phone blasted. "I gotta take this." He got up and walked away.

Into his cell phone, Frankie snapped, "Why are you calling me?"

"I want to know when you're gonna take care of our little problem," the person with the snake pinky ring inquired.

"It's not a *little* problem," Frankie barked. "She's my *sister*!"

The person retaliated, "And you better take care of *her* before *we* take care of *you*!"

****

Vinny tossed and turned in her sleep, as a large, dark car was bumping her car. She tried desperately to keep her car in the road, as the persistent person forcefully tried to run her car off the road. Tears began rolling down her face, then she lost control, and her car went tumbling over the embankment as she screamed. Vinny jumped up in the dark room in a cold sweat, and Chaz turned and spotted her in the dark, sitting up. "Honey, what's wrong?" he asked, placing his hand on her back.

"I was run off the road," she stated matter-of-factly.

"What?" he asked, sitting up and turning on the bedside lamp.

"Just before my car hit that embankment, a car crashed into me. Someone was trying to *kill* me," she explained just as they heard a large crash from downstairs. Chaz jumped out of bed first, followed by Vinny, retrieving their housecoats.

Chaz, followed closely by his wife, tipped slowly out of the room and to the top of the stairs. They witnessed Detective Harper catching a bullet from a stranger, dressed in black at the door with an extended semi-automatic 9mm Pistol. "Get back!" Detective Harper yelled, and Chaz pushed her back into their bedroom, grabbed his cell phone and called 911, while Vinny locked the door. They heard the sound of several gunshots. Chaz then reached into the closet, retrieved a Glock 19 Gen5 handgun and loaded it with bullets.

"Chaz, don't go out there," she insisted.

"I'm not leaving you," he promised. "Stay down, baby. Everything will be all right." She crotched in a corner behind the bed, and he knelt in front of her.

****

"Shelby, you're coming home later and later every night," her husband observed as she entered the house.

"Tony, you know Valencia's show is next month. I've been extremely busy," she countered. "I told you, after the show, things will settle down."

"Vinny's had shows before, and you've never been this busy."

"Well, this time she's including some of Parker's pieces, so I'm having to work twice as hard."

"Are you sure that's all that's going on?" he questioned.

"What're you getting at?"

He took a breath then inquired, "I'm getting at…do you still want this marriage or *not*?"

****

Suddenly, a banging erupted on the door as Chaz secured Vinny behind him, and simultaneously, they heard sirens approaching. "It's me," Detective Harper called, and Chaz ran to the door, followed closely by his wife. He yanked it open, and the detective stumbled in, soaked in blood. Chaz helped him to a chair and Vinny grabbed a towel from the adjoining restroom.

"Where is he?" Chaz shrieked.

"I got him," the detective confirmed just before he blacked out.

Chapter 13

Sabrina, in pink leotards, a short, white, flare dress, and pink ballet point shoes, with her hair pulled back in a ponytail, danced exuberantly to Beethoven's *Fifth Symphony* in an empty room. She was so engrossed in her routine, as she swirled, twisted, and leaped around the room until she didn't hear Parker hobble to the door, admiring her talent in blue jeans, a burgundy, plaid, button-down shirt, hanging loosely, and a blue denim baseball cap turned backward. She finally spotted Parker then leaped to him, grabbed his hand, pulled him on the floor gently as he limped in without his crutch, and proceeded to dance around him. She ended the dance with an explosive parade of pirouettes, butterfly jumps, a few jete battu leaps, a grand jete, and a grand finale of a full split to the floor. Parker smiled, clapping his hands, expressing his approval. "Beautiful," he complimented, meeting her with a kiss as she hopped up. "When is the big audition to the ballet company?"

"Next week," she shared, wrapping a towel around her shoulders, and dabbing the sweat from her face and neck. "Thank you for letting me move all your stuff to make this room suitable for me to practice."

"Well, it's the least I could do. You're here to help *me*."

"Can you come with me?"

"Where? Your *audition*?"

"Yes, for moral support."

"An audience can attend?"

"Well. You can't go into the audition, but you can go with me to the theater," she explained. "Well, can you?"

"Sure, honey, if that's what you want."

Smiling big, she acknowledged, "Thank you, baby." She kissed him deeply.

"Wow! You're welcome," he accepted, smiling with her.

"Hey, where is your crutch?"

"In the kitchen," he answered as they walked out the room. "That thing is so aggravating."

"Baby, you don't want to put pressure on your leg too soon," she advised, walking into the kitchen with him, and he sat at the small table. "I'll fix breakfast as soon as I take a quick shower and change."

As she walked out, he clicked on the small television set on the counter. His eyes widen as the news anchor reported, "Accomplished artist, Valencia Perkins and her husband, Dr. Chazmond Perkins, the principal of Bayside High School, are fine after an intruder killed the policeman who was assigned to guard Mrs. Perkins and was then killed himself by Detective Jerry Harper. Detective Harper was shot in the crossfire but is expected to recover."

"What the…" Parker breathed as he retrieved his cell phone from his pocket.

"Parker, I'm okay," Vinny blurted out.

"Where are you?"

"Chaz and I are at a hotel since the police took control of our house," she explained.

"I'm so sorry, but I'm happy you're all right."

"Thank you, Parker. I won't be at work in a couple of days."

"Sure," he acknowledged. "Do they know who did this?"

"The man was killed, but Detective Harper said he was a professional hit man."

"Oh my God! These people are *serious*!"

"It seems so."

"My God, Vinny, what did you witness?"

"I have no idea."

"You don't remember anything else?"

"No, I don't. I wish I did."

"Do you still have police protection?"

"Yes. There are two policemen at our door now," she confirmed. "Parker, I feel so bad about that policeman getting killed and Detective Harper getting shot."

"Don't think about that now, honey. It wasn't your fault," he made known as Sabrina entered the kitchen again in black shorts, sleeveless turquoise blouse, and her hair hanging wet. She frowned, wondering who her boyfriend was calling *honey*.

"Who was that?" she charged immediately when he hung up.

"Vinny," he responded, feeling offended with her tone. "She and Chaz had trouble at their house last night. A policeman was killed."

"What?!" she exploded. "Are you *serious*?! What happened?!"

****

Lying back in her husband's arms in the king-sized bed, Vinny shared, "That was Parker. He saw it on the news."

"I didn't think about it would be on the news already."

"Neither did I."

Indicating the beautiful hotel suite, Chaz recognized, "This would be nice if we weren't in danger,"

"Yes, it would," she agreed, snuggling up close to him.

"Baby, maybe you need to try hypnosis again. You've *got* to remember what happened, so we will know who's trying to *kill* you," Chaz suggested.

"I agree."

"So, you didn't see the person who was trying to run you off the road the day of the accident?" he probed, and she shook her head.

"All I saw was a big, dark car. It could have been black or dark blue. I don't know."

"It's okay, baby. We'll figure it out."

"But I do know that I didn't just *lose* control of my car. I was *run* off the road."

****

"Is she alright?" Sabrina asked Parker while they were still sitting at the kitchen table.

"Yes, thank God."

Sabrina focused on Parker hard as he sat staring into space, and she finally demanded, "Is there anything going on between you are Vinny?"

"What?!" he jerked to look at her.

"You seem very upset over someone who is *just* your employer."

"What're you talking about?" he bade, very confused with a quizzical, raised eyebrow. He knew Sabrina was insanely jealous, but he had no idea she was jealous of his relationship with *Vinny*.

"Do you have a thing for her, Parker?"

Shaking his head, Parker snarled, "I can't believe you're asking me something so stupid."

Growing upset, she snapped, "Don't call me *stupid*, Parker Grayson!"

"Then don't *act* stupid!" he retorted, losing all patience with his girlfriend. "Vinny is not *just* my employer. She's my *friend*. And if you think there is more to it than that, than you can just get the hell outta my house *and* my life!" He stood to leave, and she jumped up, grabbing his arm.

"I'm sorry," she apologized. "Please don't be angry." She hugged him tight, burying her head in his chest as tears rolled down her face. "I'm so sorry."

Parker blew hard to gain control of his temper, then raised her head with his finger and came back with, "I'm sorry for yelling at you." He planted a kiss on her forehead and took a breath. "I love you. Don't you understand that?" She nodded slowly. "Why can't you trust me?"

She sniffed and answered, "I don't know. I guess because you're so handsome. It's hard to believe someone like *you* would want *me*."

"That's just silly, Sabrina," he countered. "I could say the same thing. You are so beautiful and so talented. I feel lucky that *you* want *me*." He planted a kiss on her lips. "I love you."

"I love you too," she admitted, and they kissed again. Then he sat again and pulled her on his lap.

"Baby, you can't be jealous of every woman I encounter, especially *Vinny*. She's my boss, and we work very closely together. Vinny is like a sister to me," he explained.

"I know. Vinny is genuinely nice. It's just *me*. When my father walked out on us when I was twelve, it devastated me, and I guess it became hard for me to trust *any* man," she confessed.

"I'm *not* your father," he emphasized. "And the only thing Vinny can remember right now is how much she *loves* her *husband*. If you're worried about *anyone*, I can promise you, it shouldn't be *Vinny*." He pulled her in his arms and hugged her tight, and she felt so safe in his arms.

As Sabrina rested in his caring arms, she knew she had to get a handle on her jealousy before she lost him, and the thought frightened her.

****

"How are you, Detective?" Vinny asked as she and Chaz entered Detective Harper's flower-filled hospital room, with an arrangement of flowers for him from them.

Sitting up, he responded, "I'm great. It was just a flesh womb. I'll be leaving here tomorrow." Then he indicated the woman sitting beside his bed. "This is Carol, my wife. Carol, this is Chaz and Vinny Perkins."

"How do you do?" The red-headed lady spoke friendly, and the couple returned the warm greeting.

"Thank you for saving us," Chaz acknowledged.

"You're welcome, but it's my job," he made known.

"Well, we appreciate it," added Vinny. "I had another flashback." Detective Harper sat up even straighter to hear more. "I didn't just *run* off the road. Someone *forced* me off."

"Did you see anybody?" Detective Harper wanted to know.

"No, just a big, dark car."

"She's on the way to see her therapist now. We are hoping that hypnosis will help," Chaz offered.

"Okay. Keep me posted," the detective beckoned.

"We will," Chaz promised.

"Mrs. Perkins, I think we need to get you to a safer environment," the detective suggested. "At least until you remember everything."

"You mean to an FBI *safe house*?" Vinny chuckled, and Detective Harper nodded. "And leave my *home*?!"

"Yes," the detective confirmed.

"But I have a show coming up," she protested. "I'm not letting this maniac run me out of my house."

"Mrs. Perkins, that man was a *professional*. Whoever is trying to kill you before you remember, isn't playing!" Detective Harper stressed.

"He's right, sweetheart," Chaz added.

"But I need to finish my *work*," she insisted.

Detective Harper took a deep breath and reacted harshly, "You *need* to *stay alive!*"

****

"Have you talked to Vinny?" Justine asked her mother, as she strolled into the kitchen in a short, shirt-like, yellow floral dress with her long, micro-braids hanging loosely, where her mother in a huge, pink, floral house dress, sat at the table, peeling potatoes.

"I talked to her this morning. She's fine," her mother confirmed, as her daughter joined her at the table.

"Vinny had better hurry and remember what happened to her before some madman kills her," Justine stated, picking up a potato and helping her mother peel them.

"I'm sure she realizes that, sweetie," her mother concurred. "Hey, where's Ryan. I haven't seen him in a while?"

"That whiney, *mama's* boy!" Justine spat.

Bursting into laughter, her mother advised, "Honey, you're too young to know it now, but a *mama's* boy is a *good* catch."

"Are you *serious*?!" the young woman screamed. "Every time we want to do something, his mother always finds something else for him to do, and guess who *always* wins?"

Chuckling, her mother added, "It's not a competition, sweetheart."

"Sometimes I feel like it is."

"Justine, there's an old saying that states if a boy is good to his *mother*, he will be good to *you*, and if he's someone you want to *marry*, that's a *very* good trait," her mother explained.

"*Marry*?!" she exploded. "I can't even get him away from his *mother*!" They burst into laughter as Frankie entered with his blue jeans sagging off his hips and an oversized gray T-shirt, and his kinky, uncombed hair sticking up on his head as usual.

"Ma, you're home?" he acknowledged.

"Yeah, I'm off today," Mrs. Dow shared.

"What were you saying about Vinny?" he probed.

"There was a shooting at her house last night," his sister revealed.

"Is she alrigh'?" he inquired.

"Yeah, she's okay, and so is Chaz, but a cop was killed and one shot, but he'll be okay," Mrs. Dow explained.

"There is nothing the doctors can do to make her remember?" Justine inquired.

"Apparently not, sweetheart," her mother replied.

"She must've seen something terrible," Justine hypothesized.

"I guess so," her mother agreed, as Frankie walked out quickly, thinking that these people mean business. *Vinny was as good as dead*!

****

"What're you doing here?" Parker asked Vinny as she walked into the back room, wearing a neat turquoise Capri set with a matching band around her kinky curls, where he sat already painting.

"I have a show to get ready for. Remember?!" she joked.

"Are you *nuts*?!" he exploded. "Someone is trying to *kill* you!"

"I can't hide under a rock," she defended, pulling on a work smock.

"You don't have to be out in the *open* either," he countered, hobbling to get her supplies, in blue jeans, white T-shirt, a painter's smock, and his characteristic baseball cap turned backward.

"Where's your cane?"

Pointing to a corner, he shared, "It's right there."

"Shouldn't you be *using* it?"

"I feel okay."

"Yeah, you feel fine, the way you're hopping along," she sarcastically observed, laughing, and he laughed with her.

He sobered and added, "Seriously, Vinny, be careful. I don't want anything to happen to you."

****

Chaz sat in the large conference room in neatly pressed khaki pants and a button-down, wine-colored shirt, hanging loosely, while his leadership team entered.

"So, what's the word, Boss?" Chase inquired right away as he sat on Chaz's left side wearing a school-decorated, baseball cap, short blue jeans, and a school-decorated T-shirt.

"The board thinks the hybrid model was a huge success this year, so we will continue it next year. However, they do want us to adjust the schedule. Based on the parent and student surveys, they feel the students are on the computers too long each day," Chaz announced.

"It's good that the program is successful," added Brooke, pushing her short-cut, brown hair behind her right ear. She looked very stylish in her pale blue pantsuit covering her tanned body.

"So, will the new schedule affect the students who are attending face-to-face instruction as well?" asked Bobby, pushing his eyeglasses up on his nose.

"They want *us* to develop a schedule, so that will be up to us to decide," Chaz confirmed.

"What about *our* schedule, the leadership team?" Chase wanted to know. "Will our schedule stay the same?"

"Yes, we will work every day as usual, but I would like for each of you to take one day each week off to work at home, so you can focus on the virtual students," Chaz explained. "We know when we're in the building there is always something to do, so if you're at home, you won't be distracted."

"Do you have a schedule for us?" Brooke wanted to know.

"Yes, I do. Robin and Monica will be here every day, so I divided the days between us," Chaz explained. "Unfortunately, I won't be around too much until they catch the person who is trying to kill my wife."

"I was sorry to hear about the trouble at your house," Bobby said.

"Thank you," he replied.

"That was terrible," added Chase, removing his cap, and fluffing his twists.

"You still don't have any leads?" asked Brooke.

"Not yet," Chaz confirmed. "Bobby, can you do Mondays at home?"

"Sure," Bobby responded, removing a small pen from the pocket of his denim, button-down shirt, and a pad from his brown pants.

"Brooke, can you do Tuesdays?" Chaz went on, and she nodded. "Chase, I have you down for Wednesdays." The young man nodded. "I'll do Thursdays when things settle down with Vinny. In the meantime, I need all of you to rotate covering me on Thursdays, if that's all right?" They agreed enthusiastically. "I'll call you when I'm not going to be available, and I'll have my work cell phone on me at all times if you need me." They nodded again.

"How is Vinny?" Brooke asked.

Looking up from his paper, Chaz answered, "She's okay. Thank you for asking."

"She must be so scared," added Bobby.

"Yes, she is. As a matter of fact, we *both* are," replied Chaz. "But she still has police protection."

"I hope they catch that psycho soon," joined Chase.

"Thank you," accepted Chaz.

"What about Fridays?" asked Brooke.

"We can all manage Fridays here in the building," he answered, and she nodded. "We'll work from eight to five every Monday through Thursday during the summer." They nodded. "Brooke, how are we coming with the graduation ceremony this year?"

"Everything is fine. We only have three seniors that didn't make it, but they will be finishing in summer school," she explained. "Guidance has already contacted the students and their parents."

"Great!" Chaz acknowledged. "Bobby, would you please assemble the seniors in the auditorium after lunch?"

"Sure."

"Chase, we need the eLearning students on too, so would you please set up a Zoom link so they can join us also?" Chaz instructed.

"Done."

"Awesome," Chaz acknowledged, as Monica entered with phone messages for him. Bobby and Chase noticed that she was dressed in a pair of black slacks and a black and white silk blouse, instead of her usual seductive outfits, and they focused on each other.

When Monica was gone, Chase looked at Brooke and asked, "You did that?"

"Did what?" she chuckled.

"You know what! Tone down the voluptuous princess!" Chase laughed, and Brooke laughed with him. "You're full of it, Brooke. Now we don't have any eye candy." He continued to laugh as the rest of them joined in with his humor.

****

"Vinny!" a voice yelled from the front of the studio.

"That sounds like the beautiful Diamond Walters," Parker chuckled, as Vinny smiled and walked out front.

"I can't get pass your bodyguards," Diamond laughed, and Vinny nodded to the two policemen, then Diamond walked to her and hugged her, while the policemen focused on her legs in that short, tight, black skirt and black six-inch heels. "How are you, honey?"

"I'm okay."

"Come on. Let me take you to lunch."

"Diamond, I'm trying to finish my work."

"*Thirty* minutes!" she insisted. "You can take *that* much time for yourself, *Picasso*!"

Vinny burst into laughter. "Okay. I *am* getting hungry," she agreed. "I'll see if Parker wants to come too."

"Oh, yeah. He'll give us something *good* to look at while we're waiting on the food," Diamond chuckled.

"Down, girl. He's too young."

"Not *that* young!" she yelped. "He's what twenty-three, twenty-four? I'm *only* thirty-two."

"Stay in your lane, girlfriend," Vinny concluded, jovially, exiting into the back room. "Parker, I'm going to lunch with Diamond. Would you like to come?"

"No thank you. I'm on a roll and I wanna finish."

"Okay. I'll lock the front door," Vinny made known, and he nodded. "Would you like for me to bring you something back?"

"No, I'm good," he rejected, and as she left, he called back, "be careful! I want you back in one piece!"

****

"Chaz, I don't want to work with Brooke!" Monica announced, charging into his office.

"She's an assistant principal," he replied. "You *have* to work with her."

"No, I don't!"

"Monica, this is silly," he stressed. "You and Brooke have *got* to get along. We all work here together!"

"She's a nosy, busybody who has nothing else to do but stay in other people's business!"

"She's not like that!" he defended. "You stay in your office, and she'll stay in hers. You won't have to communicate that often."

"*Once* is too much!"

"Be nice, Monica," he suggested.

Monica blew hard then snap on her way out, "She just better stay the hell outta my face!"

****

All heads turned when Diamond strolled into the restaurant with that short, tight, black skirt, six-inch heels, and that tight, mint-green, silk blouse with her long, blonde hair hanging down her back and her makeup and jewelry so immaculate. As Vinny trailed behind her friend, she couldn't help but smile. She wondered if this woman was always so flamboyant, and if so, why were they friends. Diamond put her to shame in her little knee-length, blue jumper, sandals, and her natural hair, short and kinky.

The two policemen guarding Vinny selected a table nearby them. "Good afternoon," the waitress spoke to the ladies. "What may I get you to drink?"

"Strawberry lemonade," Vinny answered quickly.

"Martini," replied Diamond. "Very dry."

"Don't you have to go back to work?" Vinny inquired.

"No, I'm working from home the rest of the day," she made known.

The waitress acknowledged, "I'll be right back with your drinks and to take your orders."

Diamond immediately focused on her friend and inquired, "How are you doing, girlfriend?"

"I'm okay. Detective Harper wants Chaz and me to go into hiding."

"That might not be a bad idea."

"I have to finish my work for the show."

"Are you still having it?"

"Absolutely!"

"Good cause I want my *Valencia Perkins' original*."

"And you shall have it."

"Hey, don't forget about the banquet Saturday evening."

"I won't. I'm looking forward to it!" Vinny shared, then suddenly a flashback of Diamond jerking to look at her flashed before Vinny's eyes, and she glued her eyes shut, shaking her head.

Noticing her friend's expression, Diamond probed, "What's wrong?"

"I had another flashback," she confessed.

"What did you see?"

Staring at her friend, Vinny replied with raised eyebrows, "I saw...*you*."

****

"I told you she's being guarded twenty-four-seven!" Frankie insisted into his cell phone, sitting on the tree swing with his jeans sagging off her hips.

"I know. That detective took out a man that had a great reputation," the person with the snake ring replied on the telephone. "What do you suggest, Frankie. I'm not going to prison."

"*Nobody's* going to prison. I told you; she don't remember *nothing*."

"What if she starts to remember?"

"We'll cross that bridge when we get to it!"

"No, Frankie, I don't want to cross no *bridges*. I want to *eliminate* the bridge! I thought you said you were in!"

"I am, but it's hard to *kill* your own *sister*!" Frankie stressed then turned around and focused on Justine standing there with her mouth wide open.

****

"What'd you mean you saw *me*?" Diamond's voice trembled a little, nervous at the answer she might hear.

"I don't know," Vinny shook her head. "I just saw you in my flashback. You were looking at me rather surprised. I think someone was behind you, but I didn't see who it was."

"Wow! That's good you're remembering something," she replied, as the waitress brought their drinks. Diamond was happy for the interruption, to give her time to think without making her friend suspicious. She wanted to tell Vinny, but Chaz said not to, and she had to respect his wishes.

"May I take your orders?" the waitress asked.

"Club sandwich," Vinny ordered.

"Same for me," added Diamond.

"You want fries with that?" the waitress asked, and both of them shook their heads. "Okay, it'll be right up." She took their menus and left.

"What else did you see?" Diamond pressed.

"Nothing. That was all," she confirmed. "Did I see you the day of my accident?"

"Yes. We see each other practically every day."

"Was there anything different about *that* day?" Vinny wanted to know, and Diamond shook her head, taking a sip of her drink.

"I don't remember anything being different."

Vinny took a deep breath then added, "Maybe I'm just grasping at straws."

"No, it's good you're remembering *something*," Diamond coaxed. "Keep trying."

Vinny couldn't help but think that her longtime friend was hiding something. She sounded awfully nervous. *What could it be?*

****

"Good afternoon, seniors!" Chaz greeted the four hundred students in the auditorium with another three hundred on Zoom. They applauded and whooped. "You have done it!" They exploded in shouts, screams, and whistles again. When they were silent again, he continued. "Graduation is right around the corner, and we need to share some vital information with you." The administrative team and two guidance counselors began passing out folders. "You are receiving packets concerning the end of the year activities with dates and times. Do you have any questions before we get started?" A dark-skinned boy with dreadlocks in his hair raised his hand. "Yes, Darnell."

"Dr. P, does your wife have her memory back yet?"

"No, not yet, Darnell. Thank you for asking," Chaz shared as another boy with blonde hair and blue eyes raised his hand. "Yes, Halsey."

"Dr. Perkins, you have the best of two worlds."

"How so, Halsey?"

"You have a different woman without cheating on your wife," he chuckled, and the students snickers slightly. "You got it made."

"You think so, huh?" a girl sitting beside him snapped.

"I'm not talking about *me*," the boy blurted out quickly, rubbing her hand.

"That's not funny," she continued. "I know Mrs. Perkins is scared and nervous!"

"Yes, she is, Paige," Chaz confirmed.

"I didn't think…" Halsey started but the girl cut him off.

"You're right; you didn't *think*!"

"It's okay, Paige," Chaz continued. "It is very different, and my wife is *very* scared."

"Is she still having her art show next month?" another girl asked. "My dad has one of her paintings."

"Yes, she is, Leah," Chaz confirmed. "But we are getting off track. Let's get back to your graduation." The students cheered with approval.

****

Frankie hung up his cell phone then focused on Justine, who was still staring at him. "Frankie, what do you know about Vinny's situation?"

"Nothing," he snapped. "Leave me alone."

"Do you have anything to do with the shooting at Vinny's house?"

"No. Are you *crazy?!*"

"Then how are you involved?" she asked, planting her hand on her hips as she stood with tight blue jeans.

"I'm not! Just leave me the hell alone!" He barked then walked away. Justine couldn't believe her ears. Frankie could be involved with trying to kill their sister. She *had* to find out…and *soon*…before Frankie did something that he would regret for the rest of his life.

****

Chaz entered the backroom of Vinny's studio and she and Parker were cleaning up their supplies. "Hi, honey," he greeted, meeting her in a kiss.

"Hi, baby. Don't let me get this paint on you," she said holding dripping brushes back.

"Hi Parker."

"Hi, Chaz," he responded, taking the brushes from Vinny, and handing her a cloth. "I got 'em, boss."

"Thank you," she consented, dried her hands, and then hugged her husband, giving him a big kiss. "How was your day?"

"Okay."

"You look tired."

"A little."

"I'll give you a full body massage when we get to the hotel," she whispered in his ear.

"Um, that should do it," he murmured back in her ear, then kissed her lips again. "The police have finished with the house. The cleaning service is coming tomorrow, and then we can move back home."

"Great!" she acknowledged, going back to help Parker clean up.

"But I do think you need to consider getting lost like Detective Harper suggested," Chad made known.

"I will. I only have one more piece to finish before the show," she agreed.

"I'll pick up some Mexican food tonight for dinner," he suggested.

"Don't get much. I had lunch with Diamond. I'm not very hungry," she shared, and he nodded.

"I'll meet you at the hotel," he finalized then kissed her again, and she nodded. "See ya, Parker."

"Chaz," Parker recognized as he left. Then he focused on Vinny. "Get your head outta the clouds. You'll see him soon."

Vinny burst into laughter and replied, "Is it *that* obvious?"

"Yes, Ma'am," he joked. "And Sabrina's jealous of *you*."

"What?"

"Sabrina is jealous of *everyone*."

"Why? You're very devoted to her."

"Something about her father walking out on them when she was a kid, and now she has trust issues with men."

She took a breath. "She needs to get over that."

"Yeah, she does. I love Sabrina, but I don't know how much more of her jealousy I can take."

****

"Jarrick?"

"Yeah. Who's this?" he barked into his cell phone.

"This is Justine," she introduced, sitting on the bed in her pink, decorated bedroom.

"Oh, hi beautiful," he cooed, smiling wide, exposing his gold fronts. "What's up?"

"I wanted to ask you something about Frankie."

"What about Frankie?" he inquired, sitting on a couch in boxer shorts, lighting a joint with Muriel sitting beside him in a gold, lacy bra and matching panties, and her long, blonde, weaved hair secured in a ponytail.

"Did Frankie have anything to do with what happened to my sister?"

"What?!" he exploded, sitting up and passing the blunt to the young lady.

"I overheard something he said?" Justine explained. "Do you know if Frankie had anything to do with what happened to Vinny?"

"Gee, Justine, this is heavy. He didn't say anything to me. Did you ask him?"

"I did, but you know Frankie."

Chuckling, he acknowledged, "Yeah, he can be strange sometimes."

"If you find anything out, would you please call me?"

"Sure," he agreed. "I'll see what I can find out."

"Thanks, Jarrick," she completed. "I just don't want Frankie doing anything stupid that could haunt him for the rest of his life."

****

Vinny jumped up in the dark room screaming. A pounding erupted on the door, as a police officer yelled, "Is everything all right?"

Chaz turned on the lamp and investigated, "Honey, what's wrong?" She was shaking, drenched in sweat, and he called to the police officers outside the door, "Everything is okay. My wife had a bad dream." He rose from the bed and slipped into his boxers and offered, "I'll get you some water." He opened the door. The two police officers were standing at attention, waiting to hear what he had to say. "Everything's fine. She just had a bad dream."

"Yes, sir," one officer acknowledged. "Can we get you anything?"

"No, I'm just getting her some water. Thank you," he articulated. "Good night."

"Good night, sir," they said in unison, then he closed the door.

Chaz poured water in a glass and handed it to his wife. She took a small sip then handed it back to him, and he placed it on the nightstand. "Are you all right, honey?" he asked, rubbing her back gently.

"My car was going over the embankment," she cried, and he pulled her in his arms.

"It's okay, baby. You're safe," he cradled her. "You're safe."

"Why can't I remember?" she wailed. "Why can't I remember?"

"Honey, you will. It just takes time," he tried to soothe his distraught wife. "You will remember."

A terrible thought invaded her mind, so she pulled back from her husband and asked very softly, "What if I *never* remember?"

"You will," he insisted. "I promise you. You *will* remember *everything*." He pulled her in his arms again.

Gaining control of her emotions, she pulled back from his chest, looked him in the face and confessed, "I saw something else."

"What was it, darling?"

"Just as I was waking up, I saw another flashback from the night that boy was murdered," she explained. "I saw another person there."

"Who, sweetie," he coaxed. "Who did you see?"

She took a deep breath then admitted, "*Frankie*." His eyes stretched to hear more. "I think I saw my brother *Frankie*."

****

"Jackson, we need to talk," Shelby said, entering the beach house in a nice, gray, knee-length business suit, while he stood in boxers and a T-shirt, handing her a glass of red wine and keeping one for himself.

"What's wrong?" he asked, leading her into the spacious den and sitting on the couch with her.

"Honey, so much is happening to Vinny. I'm afraid she will start remembering, and I need to make things right before she does."

"Baby, we will. Trust me."

Taking a sip from her wine, she insisted, "You keep saying you got this, but I need results."

"Okay. Give me until next week."

"Are you sure?"

"Yes, honey, I'm sure," he insisted, putting his wine down and planting a kiss on her lips. "You worry too much."

"Jackson, I don't look good in orange."

"*Orange?*" he yelped. "Vinny considers you family. She would *never* put you in jail."

"I don't know," she pondered. "It's a lot."

He started massaging her shoulders. "You are so stressed. You're working so hard for Vinny. I hope she appreciates you."

"She does."

He planted a kiss on her neck and cooed, "Let me give you a back rub."

"That sounds wonderful," she agreed, enjoying the attention. "Next week, right?"

"Yes, baby," he confirmed, bathing her neck and face with kisses. "I love you. I don't like to see you so stressed."

"I love you, too," she replied, surrendering to his affections. "Please don't disappoint me again. I would die if Vinny remembered what I did."

****

Frankie and Darlene lay on a bed in the nude, smoking a marijuana joint, passing it back and forth to each other. She brushed her long, black, curly hair out of her face and turned on her stomach, exposing tattoos covering her entire back and legs. "Want another beer?" she asked him then he planted a kiss on her shoulder, dropping his arm around her waist.

"No, not right now, baby" he declined, putting the butt of the joint in an ashtray. "I want something else." He smiled wide, turning her over and covering her body with his, and she received him cheerfully.

"Don't you have an appointment tonight?"

"Not until midnight," he answered, kissing her deeply then stopping abruptly. "Darlene, do you have my stuff?"

"Yeah, baby. It's in my purse."

"Good," he acknowledged, maneuvering his body between her thighs.

Jarrick and Muriel lay asleep on the floor with a blanket covering their nude bodies. The hotel room was a mess with clothes, beer cans, cigarettes, and other drug paraphernalia filling the small, dingy room.

Darlene flipped over so that she was on top of him. She began sliding down, bathing his hard, smooth, dark body with soft, moist kisses, as he moaned his excitement.

Suddenly, a dark figure burst through the door with a semi-automatic weapon. He blasted a few rounds before tripping over the couple on the floor. Frankie seized his 9mm Pistol from the nightstand, while the girls erupted into a wail of screams as the shattering array of gunfire erupted throughout the dark room.

Chapter 14

"Hi, honey," Sabrina singsong with a ponytail in her hair, strolling into the back room of the studio where Parker sat on his stool in front of his canvas, painting.

"Hi," he beamed, meeting her with a kiss, keeping his hands away from her to avoid getting paint on her. "Where're you off to?"

"To see you," she responded, straddling her body across his lap, as her short flare skirt rose high on her thighs.

"You gonna get paint on your clothes?"

"I don't care," she snickered.

"You don't care?!" He laughed, and she shook her head, then kissed him again. "What's going on?"

"I'm *in*, baby!" she answered softly then yelled, "I'm *in*! I just got the call! I made the City Ballet company!"

"Baby, that's great!" he joined her enthusiasm, hugging her slightly, still trying to keep his paint-covered hands from touching her. "We have to celebrate!"

"Great! Where're we going?"

"I'll cook something."

"You will?!" she solicited, still smiling big.

"Of course. What do you want?"

"Anything you fix will be fine, sweetheart."

"Okay. Spaghetti it is!" he laughed. "Vinny taught me how to make a *mean* spaghetti!"

She burst into laughter and accepted, "Perfect!" Then she grew solemn.

"What's wrong?"

"Honey, we're going on tour next month."

"That's great, baby!"

She took a deep breath then asked softly, "Can you come with me?"

****

"Who was that?" Chaz asked Vinny, sitting at the breakfast nook with her while they ate breakfast.

Vinny hung up the telephone and announced, "That was Justine. Frankie got shot last night?"

"What?!" he exploded. "How is he?"

"Not good."

"Where was he?"

"In a flee-bag motel room with three other people," she announced. "Jarrick, his best friend didn't survive."

"Oh, my God!"

She stared into space then pondered, "I wonder if it had anything to do with *me*?"

"Why would it have anything to do with you, sweetie?"

"Because Frankie was there when that boy was murdered. Maybe somebody's trying to shut *him* up too."

****

"I'm dealing with stupid *morons*!" the person with the snake pinky ring raged. "How in the hell could that idiot not kill the main target, and on top of that to get killed himself!" The person took a deep breath. "I swear, if I go down, every freaking person I know is going down with me!" The person took another deep breath. "I guess I'll have to kill that bitch myself!" The person picked up a newspaper and read headlines that announced Vinny's upcoming art show. "That's it! No one would expect anything *there*. It's got to be done then...*at her show!*"

****

"How is the show coming, sweetheart?" Mayor Carson asked Shelby while they sat on the couch in the beach house, drinking wine; he was in black silk pajamas and she in a short, yellow night shirt.

"It's going great," she glowed. "Valencia's new stuff is fabulous!"

"That's awesome, sweetheart," he replied. "So, the memory loss hasn't affected her talent?"

"Not at all," she shared. "Which reminds me, baby. When are you going to take care of this place?"

"My accountant is working on it," he responded. "You know we have to be careful to keep my wife from finding out about this place."

"I know, honey, and I have to keep it from my husband as well. That's why I was concerned about..."

He turned to her, touched her chin lightly with his finger, and asked softly, "Baby, I got this!"

"I know," she came back with, and they met in a sweet kiss.

"I love you."

"Oh, Jackson, I love you so much," she made known, and they kissed long and deeply. "Why don't we just run away together to some far-a-way place and live happily ever after."

"I'll like that," he murmured between kisses. "If I don't run for mayor again, I could get a divorce." Her eyes widened.

"Are you serious?"

"Yes, I'm serious," he confirmed. "I want us to be together. I'm tired of hiding."

She beamed, "I thought you wanted to run for Governor."

"I did at one time, but I don't know now," he shared. "Maybe it's time for me to plan the second half of my life, and I want *you* in it."

****

"Sabrina, I can't go on tour with you!" Parker insisted.

"Why not?" she pressed, standing, and he stood with her. "I'll be making enough money for *both* of us."

Parker walked to the sink and began washing his hands, then insisted, "I don't want to live on *you*! I have my own career I'm trying to launch!"

"But, honey, my career has already started. You can go with me and support me with my career!"

He blew hard then stood his ground, "I can't do that. I love my work. Vinny is gracious enough to let me add my paintings to her show." He dried his hands and walked to her. "Honey, this is my big break. You just got yours. Let me have mine."

"Is that what this is all about, Parker...*Vinny*?!"

"What?!"

"Does she mean more to you than I do?"

"Sabrina, that's crazy!"

"Is it?"

"Yes!" He stressed, growing very impatient and annoyed with his girlfriend. "I told you, there is nothing between Vinny and me but a working relationship."

"But I bet you *want* more!" she accused, and he just stared at her. Parker knew Sabrina was jealous, but he had no idea just how jealous! He was tired of defending his relationship with Vinny.

"This conversation is over," he calmly finalized. "I can't believe it's lasted this long." He walked away to clean his brushes.

"Parker, this is *not* over!" she demanded.

"Yes! It *is*!" He stressed, and she touched his arm and he turned to face her again. "Sabrina, you either trust me or you don't. If not, then there's no need to continue this relationship." Her mouth flew open. She didn't see that coming.

"What?" she responded weakly.

"You heard me. If there is no trust in our relationship, then we don't have a relationship." He removed his baseball cap. "I'm tired of dealing with the same shit over and over with you. We have chosen careers that will send us in different directions quite a bit. If we can't trust each other, how can we make this work?"

She moved slowly and ended with her head in his chest, hugging him tightly and whispering so softly, he could barely hear her, "I'm sorry." He took a deep breath then reluctantly hugged her back. "I love you so much."

"Then you've got to trust me," he stated matter-of-factly. He held her head up with his finger. "Have I *ever* given you a reason *not* to trust me?" She shook her head slowly. "I'm not your *father*. I would *never* hurt you."

"Please forgive me?" she cried, unable to contain the tears flowing down her face.

He wiped her tears with his fingers, bent down and planted a soft kiss on her lips. "I forgive you as long as we *never* have this conversation again." She nodded, as he took a breath. "Now, let's go home so I can cook you that spaghetti dinner." He smiled sweetly at her, and she returned his smile. But he thought in his heart that he couldn't continue like this. Maybe it was time to let Sabrina and all her insecurities *go*.

****

Chaz and Vinny stormed into the hospital and spotted her mother, stepfather, and Justine right away. "Mom, what happened?" Vinny asked.

Wiping her tears, Mrs. Dow replied, "He was in a hotel room with Jarrick and two girls. Someone just burst in there and started shooting."

"How is he doing?" inquired Chaz.

"He's stable. He's in surgery. They took out one bullet last night, but they had to remove three more this morning," Mr. Dow explained.

"Jarrick is dead, Vinny," Justine cried, falling in her sister's arms. "He's dead. I just talked with him yesterday."

"I'm sorry, honey," Vinny tried to comfort her baby sister. "Who were the girls?"

"Darlene and Muriel," Mrs. Dow supplied. "They are fine. They had bullet wounds too, but not life threatening. They had surgery last night, so they're recuperating."

"Did they catch the person who did this?" was Chaz' question.

"He was killed also," Mr. Dow shared. "They think Frankie shot him."

"Did the girls know why he shot them?" Vinny asked cautiously.

"They didn't know him," answered Justine, sitting again.

Vinny focused on her husband, and she knew he could read her thoughts. She hoped the shooting had *nothing* to do with *her*.

****

"Hi, baby," Jake spoke, entering Diamond's condo.

"Hi," she returned, standing barefooted in a bathrobe with huge, pink curlers in her hair.

"Ready for tonight?" he asked, and she nodded. "What time do you want me to pick you up?"

"Five is good. It starts at six."

"Good, then we have time."

"Time for what?" she asked, and he took her in his arms and kissed her long.

"What do you think?"

"Oh no!" she yelped. "No time for *that*."

"There's *always* time for love, baby," he cooed, nibbling on her ear.

"No, Jake," she chuckled, pulling away from his embrace.

"Come on, baby. We have time."

"No, we don't," she insisted. "Take a cold shower."

He took a deep breath then decided to change the subject. "Is Vinny still coming?"

"I don't think so since Frankie was shot."

"That's so unfortunate," he made known, sitting at the table with her.

Handing him a cup of coffee, she agreed, "Yes, it is. Poor Vinny has had to deal with so much lately. I hope she can maintain her sanity."

****

"Mom, are you alright?" Justine asked her mother as she sat with her in Frankie's hospital room while he slept.

"I'm okay, honey," her mother responded. "Why don't you go home and get some rest."

"I don't want to leave you," she rejected as the nurse and doctor entered.

"Mrs. Dow, he's not waking up right now," the doctor revealed. "Why don't you go home and get some rest. We will call you when he wakes up."

"You removed all the bullets, right?" Patrice asked, and the doctor nodded. "Why isn't he waking up?"

"He has some swelling on his brain. He is in an induced coma so his brain will heal," the doctor explained, as Ryan entered, and Justine ran in his arms.

"How is he?" he asked.

"He's in a coma," Justine cried in his arms.

The doctor continued, "There's nothing you can do right now. He needs time to heal. You won't do him any good if you got sick."

"Come on, Mom," Justine bade. "Let me take you home. We can come back tomorrow. The police are outside the door to keep him safe." Patrice thought for a while then she finally nodded her agreement. "When Frankie wakes up, maybe he can tell us who did this."

****

Diamond exploded in smiles when she noticed Vinny and Chaz entering the exquisitely decorated ballroom. She jumped up and hugged her friend. "I didn't think you were still coming after what happened to Frankie."

"There's nothing I can do for *Frankie*, but I *can* be here to support *you*," Vinny shared.

"Thank you," Diamond responded then hugged Chaz. "Hi, Chaz."

"Hello, Diamond. Congratulations," he acknowledged.

"Thank you," she accepted. Then she introduced them to her co-workers seated at the table.

Diamond was dazzling in an expensive, red semi-formal, straight skirt suit, trimmed in sequins around the collar, cuffs and bottom of the jacket. Her silky, blonde hair hung in soft waves down her back with bumped-up bangs extending to her arched eyebrows while her neck and ears sparkled with small diamond earrings. Jake was handsomely dressed in a black tuxedo with a white shirt and black bowtie.

As Vinny watched her friend receiving accolades and giving a magnificent acceptance speech, she was extremely proud of her. She wished she could remember all the history they shared. She was glowing in a royal blue, flare, skirt suit trimmed in flowery embroidery, while Chaz rocked a black tuxedo, white shirt, and black necktie. Vinny's hair was in soft twists with pearl earrings hanging from her ears with a matching pearl necklace.

Diamond finished her speech with, "I accept this partnership with humility and humbleness, hoping that I will continue to make a difference in the firm. Thank you for the trust you are placing in me to continue the dream of this company to move it forward. God bless all of you." The room exploded with applause as she took her seat.

Jake hugged Diamond close before she took her seat and whispered in her ear, "I'm so proud of you."

Vinny met a host of people that evening who called her by name and obviously knew her. She observed how weird it was to be in a crowd of people but feeling totally alone. She felt a sense of dread as she wondered if she would *ever* get her forgotten memories back.

Part Two
One Month Later

Chapter 15

Vinny sat in their den, hanging up the telephone as Chaz entered in short khaki pants, a button-down, brown shirt hanging loosely, and brown flip-flops, with two glasses of iced tea in his hands. "How is Frankie?"

"Still in a coma," Vinny answered, receiving a glass of tea from her husband, as she relaxed in mid-thigh length, denim shorts, a navy-blue, soft-cotton blouse, and navy-blue flip-flops. Her kinky hair was encircled with a navy-blue band, and her ears were caressed with small, navy-blue earrings.

"I'm sorry," he sympathized. "It's ashamed that the guy who attacked them didn't make it either, or we could've found out something."

"I guess so."

"Do you still think this had something to do with *your* situation?"

"Yes, I do," she shared. "Justine said she heard Frankie talking to someone on the phone about not being able to kill his sister. I think the person got scared and decided to tie up all loose ends."

"That's logical, but Frankie was into the drug thing pretty heavy." he responded. "There were drugs all over that hotel room."

"And that's probably what this is all about. I don't know."

He thought for a moment then replied, "If you're right about Frankie being attacked because of you, this thing could reach very high."

"That's true," she agreed. "Detective Harper said the man was a professional hitman. Who else could afford to hire a professional *hitman* but someone with both *money* and *connections*?"

****

"Hi, Monica," Brooke addressed, entering the young woman's office. "Is Chaz coming in today?"

"I don't know," Monica nonchalantly responded, not looking up but continuing to type on her desktop.

"What did he say?" she pressed.

Monica looked up at Brooke for the first time and snapped, "Am I my brother's keeper?"

"Cute," she sarcastically reacted. "Aren't *you* his secretary?"

"We're not joined at the hip," she sarcastically retorted.

Brooke stared at the young woman long and hard before taking a deep breath, storming out and thinking, *This place isn't big enough for the two of us. Chaz is going to have to choose.*

****

"Hi, honey," Parker spoke, facetiming on his cell phone with Sabrina. "I'm glad you called. Pleasant surprise."

"Hi," she responded, smiling wide, lying on a bed in a short nightshirt, in a luxurious hotel suite. "How are you?"

"Missing you, of course," he answered. "How is everything going?"

"Going okay. I danced the lead in last night's performance."

"Look at you," he shared her enthusiasm. "I *know* you were *great*."

"I guess I was okay. I got a standing ovation."

"I'm so proud of you," he beamed. "How was the crowd?"

"Filled to capacity," she explained.

"Awesome!"

"So, how is the show coming along?"

"So far, so good!" he shared. "So, you're going abroad tomorrow?"

"How did you know?"

"Baby, I have your itinerary."

"I thought you would've misplaced it by now."

He chuckled, "See! No faith in a brutha!"

Giggling with him, she confessed, "I miss you so much."

"Baby, I never thought it was possible to miss someone so much, and you're looking sooooo good."

"So are you, honey," she agreed. "Well, I have to get ready for rehearsal. I'll call you as soon as I get to France."

"Okay, baby. I love you."

"I love you, too, sweetheart," she confided then blew him a kiss before hanging up.

Sabrina turned over on her back and stared at the ceiling. She couldn't believe how much she loved this man. She hoped he was faithful to her like he said. She would *die* if he wasn't.

****

As soon as Chaz walked into his office, Brooke entered behind him. "Hi," she acknowledged. "I wasn't sure if you were coming in today, and Monica was no help."

"I'm sorry I didn't tell you, but Monica knew," he clarified, sitting at his desk, and booting up his computer. "What's up?"

"I wanted to go over the list of summer graduates. You know we're hosting the summer graduation for all three schools this year," she explained, sitting in front of his desk.

"Yes, I know. How many do we have?"

"We have three and the other two schools have six and seven, for a total of sixteen."

"That's a good number. We can have it in the auditorium," he suggested.

"Fine," she agreed as Bobby entered.

"There he is," Bobby acknowledged. "I bought a *Valencia Perkins* original!"

"Really?" Chaz remarked.

"Actually, *Naomi* bought it."

"Great. Thank you for the support. Vinny would be pleased."

"How can *anyone* in *education* afford an original *anything*?!" Brooke joked.

"Planning, my dear," he laughed. "And marrying a penny-pinching wife helps, who can squeeze blood out of a turnip." All of them burst into laughter as Monica entered.

Totally ignoring the other two people, she handed Chaz some notes and announced, "Here are your messages."

"Thank you," he accepted, and she left just as quickly as she had entered.

"What's with her?" Bobby wanted to know.

"Oh, she's upset with *me*," Brooke answered.

"She's still mad at you for making her put on clothes?" Bobby chuckled.

"Um huh," she grunted, getting up. "I'll start on graduation with guidance, Chaz."

"Thanks, Brooke."

"And at some point, we need to talk about your *secretary*," she added as she left.

"Women!" Bobby spat. "Can't live with 'em. Can't live without 'em….well…I'll like to try." He burst into laughter.

****

"Here comes dragon lady," Parker laughed as Vinny and he cleaned their brushes, hearing the clicking sound of Shelby's heels growing nearby. Vinny laughed with him as Shelby entered the back room of the studio.

"Hi, you two!" she squealed.

"Hi, Shelby," Vinny responded first.

"What's up?" added Parker.

"Well, are you two ready for the show?" Shelby inquired.

"Yes, we are," Vinny answered.

"We're still selling pieces before the show," added Shelby.

"That's great," Vinny recognized.

"Parker, how is Sabrina?" Shelby wanted to know.

"She's good. She danced the lead last night," he responded proudly.

"Awesome!" she reacted.

"She'll be off to France in the morning."

"I know you miss her," Shelby hypothesized.

"Yes, I do."

"Will she be back for the show?" Shelby queried.

"No, she won't."

"I'm sorry, honey," she sympathized, then turned her attention to Vinny. "Any more memories coming back?"

"Not yet," she answered.

"I wish she would remember that she and I were having a wild, passionate, love affair!" Parker laughed.

"You *wish*, baby boy!" Shelby sarcastically joked, patting his cheek, and they all burst into laughter.

Chapter 16

"Vinny! Hi, sweetheart!" Grandma Eloise yelped at her door upon seeing Vinny standing there, smiling with blue jeans and a pink, button-down, silk blouse on and a pink hair band encircling her kinky hair. The two policemen guarding her stayed by the car.

"Hi, Grandma."

Her grandmother grabbed her and squeezed her tight. "It's good to see you." Vinny thought her grandmother looked very stylish in her hunter-green, capri pantsuit, soft curls in her grayish black hair, and wire-framed eyeglasses on her pecan-tanned face. "Come in."

"I hope I'm not catching you at a bad time."

"Oh no, honey. I was just watching a little television," her grandmother shared, leading Vinny into her small den and sharing the couch with her. Grandma Eloise took the television remote control and muted the sound of the news program. "How have you been, sweetheart?"

"I'm okay. Just still trying to piece together my life."

"You still don't remember anything, honey?" Grandma Eloise inquired, and she shook her head. "Don't worry. It'll come back to you." Vinny nodded. "How's Chaz taking this?"

"He's very supportive."

"That's good. You need that now," observed her grandmother as a medium-height, dark-chocolate tanned man entered in khaki pants and a brown, button-down, loosely hanging shirt, white sneakers, and his head shaved bald with a neatly trimmed beard and mustache.

"Hi, niecy niece!" he joked, pulling her up and hugging her tight. "How is life on the other side of the tracks?"

"Vinny, this is your Uncle Michael," Grandma Eloise introduced.

"Oh, it's like that, huh?!" her uncle chuckled.

"I told you the child has amnesia!"

"Oh snap!" he sobered. "So, you don't remember *anything*?"

Shaking her head, she replied, "I'm afraid not."

"So, you don't remember I owe you a thousand dollars?!" He burst into laughter, and Vinny laughed with him. "Just kidding! Don't think I'm giving you a thousand dollars, Niecy!"

"So, how is your show coming, honey?" Grandma Eloise asked her.

"It's coming great. Thank you. I hope you'll be there," she answered. "*Both* of you."

"Oh, no, I don't *ever* attend those things!" her grandmother chuckled.

"And I don't have a tux," he laughed again. "Hey, I'll catch you later, Niecy." He hugged her again. "Good luck."

"She doesn't need luck," Grandma Eloise protested. "She just needs God."

"Whatever, Ma. See you," he finalized, exiting.

"Bye, Uncle Michael," she called back, as he left. Vinny liked her uncle's energy. "Does Uncle Michael live with you?"

"Yeah, *unfortunately*," Grandma Eloise laughed then took Vinny's hands. "Come on, honey, let me pray for you." Vinny nodded. "No matter what anyone says, just remember that all you need is God. He will fix this for you."

****

"Hi Parker!" a soft voice called, and Parker looked around from the counter and spotted Justine sitting alone under an umbrella at the outdoor bistro. He couldn't help but to admire her, looking so cute in her short flare black denim skirt and sleeveless black, floral, off-the-shoulder blouse, short enough for her belly button to be exposed, and her long braids in a neat ponytail, seeming oblivious to all the men's adorning eyes.

"Justine!" he acknowledged, smiling, and she thought her heart would melt. He was so tall and handsome, with those blue jeans fitting his athletic body to perfection, accented by his short-sleeved, button-down, white shirt hanging loosely and a baseball cap turned backward on his beautiful, curly, black hair, seeming oblivious to all the admiring pairs of female eyes. "How are you?"

"Fine. Thank you."

"What's a beautiful, young woman like you doing dining *alone*?"

"My boyfriend stood me up...*again*. He had to take his *mommy* to visit his grand ma-ma," she smirked, dripping with sarcasm. "And *you*?"

"Well, my girlfriend is on tour for a few months."

"What kind of tour?"

"Dance tour. She's a ballerina."

"Wow! That sounds interesting," she returned. "Hey, I have an empty seat to share if you'd like to join me."

"Sure," he accepted. "I was going to get take-up, but it would be much nicer to dine with *you*." He thought, *If this girl wasn't my boss' sister, I might be in trouble.*

"Great!" she acknowledged as she thought, *Wow! If he wasn't working for my sister, I might be in trouble.*

****

"Hi," Vinny spoke to her dad on a telephone, looking through the glass, and sitting opposite him on the other side of the glass.

"Hi," he replied. "You look good."

Rubbing her kinky hair, still with the pink band around it, she responded, smiling, "Thank you." She didn't think she looked any different, just normal in the same blue jeans and pink silk, button-down blouse she wore to see her grandmother earlier. "You look well," Although Vinny didn't have a spark of remembrance, looking at this pathetic looking man in the orange jumpsuit, straggly beard, and bushy hair, who was her father, she hated seeing him in this place, but that was his choice.

Indicating the two policemen standing at the door, he remarked, "I suppose Frick and Frack are with you?" She nodded, and he jeered. "I hear ya, *Oprah Winfrey*!" She had to smile at that comment.

Sobering, she asked, "Dad, do you need anything?"

"No. I'm okay. Thank you."

"You know if you do, all you have to do is ask."

He nodded then inquired, "I heard on the news that you lost your memory. Is that true?"

"Yes, it is."

"So, you don't remember *me*?" he questioned, and she shook her head. "Then what're you doing here?"

"What'd you mean? You're my *father*."

"Vinny, you don't have to keep coming here," he stated. "Just to satisfy some sort of obligation."

"I didn't come out of obligation. I came because I wanted to see you."

"Why? You don't even know who I am."

"I don't know who *anyone* is, including *myself*, but I can't let that cause me to distance myself from *everyone*."

He smiled for the first time then acknowledged, "You're a good girl, Vinny. You always have been."

"Thank you," she accepted, smiling back. "So, why didn't you marry my mother?"

"I wasn't in love with her, and besides, she was only *fifteen*."

"Why would you sleep with a fifteen-year-old girl?"

"She didn't look fifteen," he defended. "She told me she was eighteen. And *I* wasn't the only one."

"Mom had another boyfriend at *fifteen*?"

"Vinny, I hate to disillusion you about your mother, but she had traveled around the block a few times before I met her."

"Mom?!" she yelped, trying to keep her voice low.

"Yes, your *mother*," he confirmed. "As a matter of fact, she was a little *slut*!"

****

Justine was riding Parker like a stallion in his king-sized bed. They were moaning and groaning until they had an explosive exchange together. Then she collapsed on his smooth, strong, muscular body and he rubbed her back softly. Finally, she blew hard and rolled off him, and landed on her back beside him. "Whew! That was incredible!" she breathed.

Catching his breath also, he agreed, "Yes, it was. Too bad this can't happen again."

"I know," she replied then chuckled, "I can't believe it happened *this* time."

"Neither can I," he laughed with her. "I guess loneliness *can* bring people together."

"I guess so."

"Want something to drink?"

Holding up on one elbow over him, she responded, "Whacha got?"

"Well, since you're not old enough to drink, I can offer you water, tea, or milk!"

"*Milk*! *Seriously*!" She burst into laughter then added, "Hey, if I'm old enough to be in bed with a gorgeous man, I'm old enough to *drink*."

"Really?" he cooed, pulling her down in a kiss. "I could get used to this."

"So could I," she agreed, as he rolled on top of her.

He kissed her lips then just stared at her. "You are so beautiful." She just smiled sweetly. "And those dimples are simple adorable."

"That's what Vinny always says."

"She's right," he agreed then kissed her again. "Vinny would kill me if she knew I was in bed with her little sister."

"I'm not that *little*, Parker. You're only a couple years older than I am."

"Yes, but the way Vinny talked about you before her accident, you seemed so much younger."

"Did she talk about me a lot?"

"Yes. All the time. She's enormously proud of you."

"And I her," she admitted then smiled sheepishly. "So, *I won't tell if you won't*."

****

"My *mother* isn't a *slut*," Vinny defended.

"I didn't say she *is* a slut. I said she *was* a slut," he stressed. "People do change."

"How would you know anything about my mother?! You were in prison before she graduated from high school!"

"I grew up in this town. People talk."

"You were twenty-five years old! You took advantage of a child!" she insisted.

"I told you. I didn't know she was that young!"

"But you knew she was a *slut*!"

"As I said, people talk, especially *men*!" He paused to give her time to absorb what he was sharing. "Vinny, all I'm saying is that there were other men who could have claimed to be your daddy!"

"What?!" she squealed. "What are you saying? You went to jail for statutory rape."

"Only because I got *caught* with her," he explained. "We never had a paternity test done. I was in prison when you were born, and she just named me because I was the one who was caught with her."

"Dad, what're you saying?"

He took a deep breath then shared, "I'm saying that although I have always loved you, I never knew if *I* was your daddy…or *not*!"

****

"Justine!" her mother called when her daughter tried to tip-toe into the house.

"Ma, what're you doing up?"

"Waiting for you."

"Why?"

Her mother patted the seat on the couch beside her, and Justine sat. "Ryan came over, looking for you."

"He did, huh?"

"Yes, and until he came, I thought you were with *him*."

"He stood me up…*again*."

"Then who were you with until two o'clock in the morning?"

"I was with a friend, Ma."

Mrs. Dow took a deep breath then stared her daughter in the eyes and admitted, "I don't even want to know who he was, Justine."

"Who said it was a *man*?"

"Honey, *been* there, *done* that!" Her mother stressed, and Justine just dropped her head. "Sweetheart, Ryan is a good man. He loves his mother, and he loves *you*." She paused and lifted her daughter's head with her finger. "Justine, do you love Ryan?"

"Yes, but…"

"No *buts*! If you love him, you must put up with the *good* as well as the *bad*," her mother explained. "Honey, your reputation is all you have. Don't ruin it." Justine's eyes widen. "Be patient with Ryan. His mother is all he has. He doesn't know if *you'll* be there for the long haul, but he knows *she* will." Mrs. Dow took a deep breath. "You are a beautiful young lady. Men will use you if you let them. You think it's because they care about you, but they're just using you for their own selfish needs." She paused again. "I don't want you to make the same mistakes I made, getting pregnant at fifteen, and having to work dead-end jobs for the rest of my life." She paused. "Your father was the best thing that happened to me. I was blessed that he looked beyond my faults and accepted me for *me*." She lifted Justine's head again. "Are you hearing me, honey?"

"Yes, Ma," she finally replied.

"If Ryan isn't the one, then let him go. Don't string him along like a little puppet."

"I'm not doing that?"

"Aren't you?" her mother countered, raising and inquisitive eye. "You weren't with him tonight." Justine began biting on her bottom lip. She knew her mother was right.

"Ma, I do love Ryan. I just get so mad when he breaks a date with me for his *mother*."

"Be patient. He's smart. He's young. One day, he'll be able to draw the line between cutting the apron string with *her* and tying a new knot with *you*."

"Do you think so?"

"Yes, I do. But only if he feels that he can depend on you, and you're not answering your cell phone all night when he called you doesn't tell him that he can," her mother explained. "What if he was in trouble or sick or *something* and *needed* you, and you were somewhere with another man *pouting*."

"I wasn't *pouting*."

"Well, I don't wanna know what *else* you were doing until two o'clock in the morning," her mother blurted out in laughter, and her daughter laughed with her.

"I love you, Ma."

"I love you too, honey," Mrs. Dow finalized, pulling her daughter in her arms, and hugging her lovingly. "Now, you call Ryan tomorrow and apologize." Justine nodded, thinking how lucky she was to have a mother that was so understanding that she could talk to like a friend.

Justine remembers hearing a preacher say one time that if a person hadn't gone through anything, that person couldn't preach to him. She thinks it was Bishop T. D. Jakes, but she wasn't sure. Her mother had lived a life that she didn't want her daughter to repeat, and Justine was thankful for her. She knew it was a one-time thing with Parker, and she didn't want to ruin what she had with Ryan for the fulfilment of a fantasy. Although she had to admit, Parker was *everything* she thought he would be, patient, romantic, and exciting. Sabrina was a lucky woman. Justine had to admit that she was lucky also. Ryan had all those qualities too, with one exception, she loved him, and that made it even better. Love does conquer all, and she was hoping that one day it would conquer a pathetic, controlling mother like Mrs. Henry.

Part Three

July

Chapter 17

"The *big* day!" Chaz identified, standing in only boxer shorts, hugging Vinny from the rear as she stood in the mirror in a short nightshirt.

"Yes, it is," she responded, dropping her head back in his chest.

"I know Parker is excited with his pieces on display for the first time."

Turning to face her husband, she responded, "Yes, he is."

"I'm happy for him," he remarked, then planted a kiss on her lips. "Detective Harper is arranging police protection, and the two policemen protecting you here will be there."

"I think I'll be okay."

"You still haven't told Detective Harper that Frankie was there when that boy was murdered?"

"No. Since Frankie's still in a coma, I didn't see where it would've helped," she explained. "And what if I'm wrong? All these young boys look so much alike with the baggy clothes and crazy hair. It may not have been Frankie at all."

"I guess you're right," he accepted. "Are you nervous about tonight?"

"A little, but I'm coping," she recognized then planted a kiss on his lips.

Pulling her closer, he hypothesized, "You'll be all right." He kissed her again, this time more deeply. "Um, it's early. Let's go back to bed," he cooed, bathing her neck with kisses.

"Sorry, I don't have time," she laughed. "Diamond is picking me up to go to the beauty shop."

"Your hair looks fine," he insisted, dropping his boxers.

Vinny licked her lips at seeing her husband's strong, smooth, lean, muscular, dark-chocolate body then chuckled, "*Oh, the heck with my hair!*"

****

Justine exploded into the kitchen with tight blue jeans on, an off-the-shoulder, button-down, sky-blue blouse that reached just above her belly button, with her natural hair, ballooning out in kinky curls just above her shoulders, where her mother was washing dishes in a floral house dress and announced, "Mom, the hospital just called. Frankie's coming outta his coma!"

"What?!" her mother screamed as Mr. Dow entered. "Oh, thank God!"

"What's going on?" he asked.

"Frankie's coming out his coma!" Mrs. Dow yelled, pulling the scarf off her head. "Let's get to the hospital!"

"I'm meeting Vinny at the beauty shop," Justine replied. "I promised Shelby I would help at the show this evening. Please tell Frankie I will see him tomorrow."

"Okay, sweetheart," her mother replied. "I can't wait to see my baby!"

"*I'm* the baby!" Justine jovially yelled back as her parents dashed out of the kitchen.

****

"Coming!" Vinny yelled, running to the door, in blue jeans, a button-down fuchsia blouse that reached her waist, and one inch heeled, strapless blue sandals.

"Come on, girlfriend, chop shop!" Diamond exploded into the house in laughter. "We gotta get moving! Time is ticking away!" She was her normal stylish self, in skin-tight, black leggings, turquoise, silk blouse that reached a little above the waist, long, hooped earrings with matching necklace, and six-inch heels. Her make-up was flawless with bright-red lipstick and her weaved blonde hair was in a neat ponytail.

"I'm ready," Vinny chuckled.

"I bet you are," her friend joked. "Can't let that tall, dark handsome man go, huh?!" Vinny laughed with her. "I ain't mad at cha, girlfriend!"

"Hi, Diamond," Chaz entered in neat black jeans, tan and black button-down shirt, hanging loosely and black sneakers.

"Hi handsome," Diamond joked, and he smiled.

"I'll see you soon, honey," Vinny verbalized as he met her in a sweet kiss.

"I have a few things to do at work, and then I'm going to help Shelby with the movers as they gather your paintings to take to the gallery," he made known, and she nodded, and then they kissed again. "See you soon."

****

"Frankie, honey, can you hear me?" Mrs. Dow asked, standing over her son's hospital bed with her husband, a doctor, a nurse, Detective Harper, and two other policemen.

Frankie opened his eyes slowly, focused on his mother and replied very weakly, "Hi, Mom."

"Oh God, thank you!" she burst into laughter.

"How are you, son," his father added.

"Hi, Dad," Frankie responded again, sounding a little stronger.

"His prognosis looks promising" the doctor shared. "No paralysis and no apparent memory loss."

"Can we ask him some questions?" Detective Harper asked.

"Keep it short," the doctor ordered.

"Frankie, do you remember what happened?" he asked, and Frankie nodded. "Do you know why you were attacked?"

Frankie took a deep breath then answered, "No."

"So, you have no idea who tried to kill you?"

"No. I ain't done nothing to nobody," Frankie continued. Frankie was not about to tell on *anybody* until he knew for sure that this had to do with the fact that he wouldn't kill his sister. "What did Jarrick say?"

His mother took his hand then shared, "Honey, Jarrick didn't make it."

"What?" he yelped, feeling hurt that he had never experienced before. If he were the cause of his long-time friend's death, he would never forgive himself. "Jarrick is dead?"

"Yes, honey," his mother confirmed. "I'm sorry?"

"What about...?"

"The girls are fine," his mother finished his thought.

"Frankie," Detective Harper added. "Are you sure you don't know the man who attacked you?"

"No, I've never seen him before that night?" Frankie admitted. Then it occurred to Frankie that Vinny still couldn't remember, or she would've told them that he was in that alley when Kenneth was murdered, and they would be asking him about that too.

"Okay, gentlemen, he needs to get some rest now," the doctor spoke up.

"Frankie, we'll be outside the door," one of the other policemen said, and Frankie nodded, wondering if they were there to protect him or to arrest him for all the drugs they found in the hotel room.

****

"Vinny, are you ready for tonight?" the lady asked Vinny as she gave her a manicure.

"I think so," she replied. "But I'm a little nervous."

Sitting in the booth beside Vinny, getting her nails done, Diamond shrieked, "*She's* fine, Jackie! Her *friends* are wrecks!" All the women laughed.

"Have you ordered your *Valencia Perkins' original* yet, Jackie?" chimed in Justine, sitting on the other side of Vinny, getting her manicure.

"Are you kidding?!" the dark-chocolate lady who was working on Vinny's nails screamed. "Girl, ten thousand dollars gotta last me more than for just *one* purchase!" The ladies all laughed. "I got three hungry little brats to feed, and they eat like food is going outta style!"

Laughing, Justine replied, "You have this lovely shop." She indicated the upscale immaculately decorated black and gold shop, where all the workers wore black smocks with their names written in gold on the left pocket, and the name of the shop written in gold on the back. "I'm sure you can afford a *Valencia Perkins' original*. It's a great investment!"

"Okay, then *you* buy me one, Miss Nurse!" Jackie continued to laugh.

"Nurse *student*!" Justine jovially corrected.

"I hear ya, girlfriend," Jackie finalized. "Vinny, how about a bright red jell color?"

"Too wild!" Vinny yelped.

"Yeah, do it, Jackie!" added Diamond. "We gotta bring this chick out a little."

"No," Vinny laughed.

"This is *your* night, girlfriend! Live a little!" Diamond insisted.

"Yeah. Hook her up, Jackie!" added Justine.

As the women chatted, laughed, and joked, Vinny felt so out of place. She had no idea who these women were or what she liked or didn't like. She had to rely on strangers to tell her what she liked. It was all so strange, and she felt drastically out of place. She had to smile and try to be involved in the conversations, but she really felt like crying. Vinny thought to herself, *Oh God, when will this nightmare end?*

****

"Is everything set for tonight?"

"Yes," the person with the snake pinky ring replied over the telephone.

"Can it be traced back to us?"

"No way. It will be clean and untraceable."

"So, tonight is *definitely* the night?"

"Yes. After tonight, we won't have any more loose ends," the person with the snake pinky ring replied. "Valencia Perkins will sponsor her last art show. Tonight, she will be put out of business…*permanently*!"

****

"Chaz, I need your signature on the paperwork for this purchase order?" Monica requested, handing Chaz the paper while he was sitting at his desk.

"What's it for, Monica?" he inquired, standing.

"Printing supplies, like ink, paper, etc."

"Oh yeah, for the admin team and office staff," he remembered, signing the paper, and she nodded.

As Chaz received the paper from Monica, she slid her finger across his hand and smiled. "Chaz, why don't you look at me like all the other men?" she cooed, looking into his deep, brown eyes. Chaz was speechless. He just stood there with his mouth drooped open.

"What?" he finally asked when he found his voice again.

Monica blew hard then confessed, "You know how I feel about you."

"Monica, you are a very attractive woman, but I'm happily married," he insisted, stepping back a little.

"She doesn't have to know."

"But *I* would know," he insisted. "I love my wife."

Monica just stared at him for a moment, then she smiled and retreated, "Okay. You can't blame a girl for trying." Then she strolled out, swaying her hips from side to side in her knee-length, skin-tight skirt. He smiled, shook his head, blew hard, then dropped in his chair again.

Chaz knew he shouldn't have asked Monica to come in on a Saturday to finish the office inventory, but it was due Monday, and he had been out of the office quite a bit with Vinny, and the paperwork had to have his signature. He was glad they were finished before she started her little attempt to lure him. He didn't want any problems. And besides, he had to get to the studio to help Shelby. Still, he couldn't believe some people. He knew Monica was a flirt, but he really didn't know she had the hots for him like that. Women were right. Men are naïve, idiots, or just plain ole *dump*!

****

"Frankie, I'll see you tomorrow, honey," his mother shared, bending down to kiss his forehead while he lay in the hospital bed. "I promised to help at Vinny's show."

"No problem, Mom," he replied.

"I'll be back to sit with you a while, son," his father shared. "Since your mother and I rode together, I need to take her home, but I'll be back. Do you want me to bring you some food back?"

"No, I'm good," admitted Frankie, and his father nodded.

"I'll send you some lasagna," his mother added, and Frankie nodded again. She reached into her purse and handed him a program. "Here, honey, this is the brochure for Vinny's show tonight. Look at the guest list. It's very impressive!"

"Thanks, Mom," he accepted, while he hoped his sister would be safe tonight at her show. It would be ashamed to get killed at such an important event. He pondered silently, *Would they actually kill Vinny at her own Art Show?*

Chapter 18

Chaz stood in their foyer, looking very handsome, debonair, and suave in a black tuxedo, black shoes, white shirt, and black bowtie, waiting for Vinny. His hair was cut low and neat with soft, smooth waves. "Honey, are you almost ready? The limousine is here!" he called. "You don't want to be late."

Suddenly, Chaz's mouth dropped open as Vinny stepped into view with a big smile, adorned in a rose-colored, straight, chiffon evening dress that handed atop three-inch glass-sequined slippers with rose-colored sparkles. The dress was accented by an open left arm and draping down on the right arm in a flare of chiffon and sequins, similar to a wedding veil. The split running up the left leg with sequins on both sides ended in the middle of her pecan-tanned thighs, which were covered by a sheer flesh-tone pair of pantyhose. The dress sparkled with sequins around the tail and neckline with small sparkling rose-colored flower petals accenting the waist down to the tail. Her ears were caressed with small, diamond studs. "Wow!" he finally spoke, and she smiled, exposing her pearly white teeth, surrounded by a light coat of makeup accenting her pecan-tanned face and a thin coat of light rose-colored lips. Her silky-smooth hair hung just below her shoulders in a silky, bouncy wrap. "Baby, you look gorgeous."

"Thank you," she accepted. "You look very handsome yourself."

"Thank you," he replied. "Ready?" She nodded, then retrieved a small sequined, rose-colored purse from the table. "This evening should be a *blast*!"

****

"Ryan," Mrs. Henry called, entering her son's bedroom, where he was standing in a black tuxedo, in front of the mirror, tying his bowtie.

"Hi, Mom."

"Hey. I thought we could grab a bite to eat. We rarely have time to spend together," she announced. "But I see you have plans."

"Mom, you know this is the night of Vinny's big show. You were invited too. Remember?" he chuckled.

"Oh, I forgot."

"No, you didn't. I reminded you last night, but you said you wanted to spend a quiet evening at home."

"I didn't know you were still going."

"Why wouldn't I?"

"Because I thought you wanted to spend some time with me."

Turning to face his mother, Ryan took a breath and inquired, "Mom, why don't you like Justine?"

She chuckled, "I didn't say I didn't like her."

"You didn't have to. Your actions speak volumes."

"I'm sorry to bother you!" his mother snapped. "If she means more to you than I do…" She turned to leave, but he caught her arm.

"Mom, you know that isn't true," he made known. "You know how much I love you, but I love Justine too. And if I keep breaking dates with her to spend time with you, I'm going to lose her." He took a deep breath. "Mom, I will always be your son, and I will always be here for you, but I have to live my own life." He paused. "Please understand."

She blew hard then stated, "I'm sorry, Ryan. You are a good boy, and I have been unfair to Justine."

"All I ask is that you give her a chance. You'll find that Justine is a genuinely nice person, and she wants to be a nurse just like you, so you two have something in common," he explained then smiled. "I love you, Mom. Nothing will *ever* change that." She nodded and he pulled her in his arms.

When Ryan released his mother, she wiped a few tears from her face then chuckled, "Does she have to go half-naked all the time?"

He burst into laughter and replied, "Mom, it's a new day." He paused. "Besides, I saw some of your old pictures. You and your sorority *sistahs* dressed the same way back in the day, or have you forgotten that?!" She burst into laughter with her son.

****

The beautifully decorated gallery was well adorned with Vinny's and Parker's paintings. The evening went very well. Shelby scheduled the time from six to nine o'clock. Shelby was in her characteristic long, flare, red evening dress, adorned with gold satin buttons down the front, and gold satin accents around the shoulder-length sleeves and collar, ending with three-inch, gold, satin pumps. Her makeup and hair were immaculate, with her hair pinned behind her left ear and her ruby-red lipstick covering her small lips. Her husband was outstanding in his black tuxedo, neatly trimmed hair that almost camouflaged his bald spot.

Mrs. Dow arranged for catering from the restaurant with waiters and waitresses to serve. They were eloquently attired in both black slacks and black shirts with white aprons.

Justine served as the greeter in her above-the knee crème colored formal, lace dress that was secured around the waist with a silk ribbon-like belt. Her open-toe, crème-colored, six-inch, silk pumps caressed her small feet with crème-colored designer-knit pantyhose. Her hair was weaved in an auburn, mask of loose-curly waves, hanging to the middle of her back with a part in the center above her forehead. Her makeup was flawless with slightly red lips, long add-on eyelashes and arched eyebrows. She handed everyone a brochure and made sure they knew how to bid on paintings.

As Vinny passed by her sister, she patted her shoulder and stated, "You look very beautiful, Justine."

"Thank you, sis. So do you," she accepted, as Vinny walked away, entering the crowd.

"You look beautiful," Parker admired Vinny.

"Thank you," she recognized. "You're not too shabby yourself.

Parker stood handsome and tall with his curly black hair cut short, his black tuxedo, black sneakers, black collarless shirt with no bowtie and no cummerbund. He missed Sabrina, but he knew she was extending her career, just like he was. Then he walked over to Justine at the door, and whispered in her ear, "You look absolutely breathtaking!"

She turned, smiled, and responded, "Thankyouverymuch!" She chuckled. "You look very chic yourself."

"Thank you," he acknowledged. "Where is the *boyfriend*?"

"Running late as usual."

"Mommy Dearest again?"

"You got it!" she laughed as guests entered. "Gotta go!" He nodded as she walked away to greet the guests.

During the evening, Vinny and Parker circulated, socializing with their guests. In the middle of the evening,

Vinny and Parker each gave a small speech, expressing gratitude, which was well deserved because the people were buying plenty. Shelby had invited the richest people she could think of, including governors, mayors, senators, congressmen, business owners, etc., and they all came. Shelby hired both a photographer and a videographer to capture every memorable moment.

Justine greeted the last group entering, and just as she was about to close the door, she spotted Ryan rushing up the walkway, looking so handsome in his black tuxedo. She smiled wide. "You made it."

"Of course, I did," he replied, planting a kiss on her cheek.

"You look beautiful."

"Thank you," she accepted. "I'm glad you're here."

"Where else would I be?" he made known, and Justine knew without a shadow of a doubt that she loved this man. She didn't know why she hadn't seen it before. She guessed she was a little jealous of his mother, but she was happy that his mother loved him so much.

"Hello, Ryan," Vinny greeted. "I'm glad you could come."

"Thank you, Vinny," he responded. "It looks like a huge success."

"I think it is" she replied, as Chaz walked to her.

"Shelby did a wonderful job," he remarked to his gleaming wife.

"Yes, she did," she replied, receiving a soft kiss on her cheek from her husband.

Diamond and Jake entered, a very handsome couple. His tall, lean body was covered in a black tuxedo, but instead of having a white bowtie and cummerbund like the other men, his was deep purple to match Diamond's formal, deep purple, long dress with matching deep purple, sequined six-inch pumps. Her dress was a silk, body fitting, off the shoulders, sparkling array of loveliness that ballooned at the feet in pop-up sequined flowers, as well as along the neckline, with the dress drooping in the back to expose her light-brown smooth skin. Her long, blonde hair was freshly weaved and hanging down her back, with her neatly cut bangs accenting her dangling, diamond earrings and matching necklace. She carried a small sequined, deep purple purse in her hand. "Vinny, everything looks wonderful!" Diamond raved.

"Thank you," she accepted, as Chaz and Jake greeted each other.

"Congratulations, Vinny," added Jake to her.

"Thank you, Jake," Vinny smiled as he kissed her cheek.

"Come on, baby, let's see what we can buy," Diamond suggested to Jake, then focusing back on Vinny and Chaz. "We'll talk later." Vinny nodded as they walked away.

"There is Mayor Carson and his entourage," Chaz acknowledged. "Shelby didn't miss anyone."

"Thank God!" Vinny praised, as the mayor and his wife walked to them.

"Congratulations, Mrs. Perkins," Mayor Carson greeted, with Tammie, his wife and his two aids, Liam, and Elijah right beside him. Tammie's petite frame was adorned in a nice, pale blue evening dress outlined by sequins, which fit her small body like a glove and mermaiden at the bottom. Her hair was pinned up in a neat bun, encircled with a diamond wreath. Shelby felt a knot in her stomach at seeing her lover with his pretty wife. She wanted to just grab him, kiss him hard, and let the whole world know that they were in love.

"Thank you, Mayor Carson," Vinny accepted. "It was so nice of you to come."

"We wouldn't have missed it," he added.

"Everything looks lovely, Mrs. Perkins," the mayor's wife commented.

"Thank you, Mrs. Carson," Vinny accepted.

"Well, we'll talk later. I want to look around," announced the mayor.

"Please," Vinny encouraged as they walked away.

Mrs. Dow walked to Vinny and Chaz and handed them each a glass of sparkling water and said, "Here, honey. You two must be thirsty."

"Thanks, Mom," she accepted, as he planted a kiss on his mother-in-law's cheek. Vinny took a sip just as the photographer asked to take a picture of her with her husband. "Sure." She and Chaz placed their drinks on a table behind them. While they took the picture, the person with the snake pinky ring passed by, dropped a small pill in Vinny's drink without breaking a stride. After Vinny and Chaz took the picture, they picked up their drinks again.

****

"How are you, Frankie?" a nurse greeted cheerfully in a distinctive accent, walking in his room, pushing a rolling cart.

"Fine, Penny. Thank you," he replied to the dark, Nigerian woman as he sat up.

"I need to take your vitals and administer your medicine, handsome," she announced, and he nodded. She placed a thermometer in his mouth and held his wrist. She noticed the brochure on his desk. "Oh, yeah, it's your sister's big day. I'm sorry you can't be there." He smiled at her. "But you're doing great. You'll probably be leaving here in the morning." She removed the thermometer from his mouth. "98.6. Great." Then she began putting the blood pressure cup around his arm. Soon she removed it and said, "120 over 78. Very good." She handed him a small plastic cup with two pills. "One of these is a pain killer, so you can rest tonight, and the other one is an antibiotic to prevent infection." He dropped them in his mouth and received the water she handed him in another small plastic cup.

Nurse Penny put everything back on her cart then picked up the brochure. "This is going to be nice." As she flipped through the pages, she asked, "Anything I can get you, Frankie?" He shook his head. "Wow! All the big dogs will be there tonight." He smiled as she replaced the brochure on the table. "I'll be here until seven in the morning. Let me know if I can do anything for you."

"Thank you," he replied, as she smiled and left.

Frankie picked up the brochure as his father entered. "Hi, son."

"Hi, Dad."

"Sorry it took me so long. I had to help your mother get the stuff ready for the show."

"No problem. I'm fine."

"Everything looked really nice at the gallery."

Flipping through the brochure, Frankie remarked, "I can tell." Suddenly, he jumped forward with outstretched eyes. "Oh my God!"

"What's wrong?" his father wanted to know, as Frankie started leaping out of bed. "What is it?"

"Dad, we gotta get to that show," he insisted, pulling on his clothes.

"Why? You can't leave the hospital! You had surgery!"

"Dad, Vinny is in danger!"

"What?!"

Frankie took a deep breath then stressed, "Dad, if I don't get to that show, Vinny will be *murdered*!"

****

When Vinny turned, she spotted the snake pinky ring on a person standing close to her, and she lost her balance, dropping her drink. Chaz caught her limp body just before she hit the floor. "Honey, what is it?" he asked.

Part Five

Back to the Past: Three and a Half Months Earlier

Chapter 19

"Hi, Parker," Vinny spoke as she entered the back room of her studio where Parker was painting on a canvas, with a du-rag on his head.

"Hi," he acknowledged. "Your stuff is ready for you."

"Thank you," Vinny replied, walking to a filling cabinet. "What time is that girl coming for the interview?"

"Four o'clock."

"It's going to be hard to replace Carmen," she added, looking through papers.

"Yes, it is."

"I hope this girl is good. We need a receptionist so bad."

"Yeah, we do."

"Did Shelby bring the inventory from my last show?"

"Yeah. They should be in there," he responded, indicating the filling cabinet. "She said the figures were impressive again."

"Great!" she recognized, looking at the paperwork. When she was about to put on her smock, her cell phone rang. "Hello? Vinny Perkins." Pause. "Thank you. I appreciate your support." Pause. "I'm sorry. What was that?" Pause. "Sure. Thanks again." She hung up and stared into space.

"Anything wrong?" Parker inquired, but her thoughts prevented her from hearing him. "Vinny?"

Shaking her head, she replied, "Fine." She took the paperwork and started for the door.

"Where're you going?"

"I'll be right back. I gotta check something out," she countered, and soon he heard the front door open and close.

****

"Vinny!" Diamond called, entering their house.

"Diamond!" Chaz exploded, entering with a towel wrapped around the lower part of his nude body. "I thought you were Vinny. I heard the car and opened the door for her.

Laughing, she said, "Sorry to disappoint you." She noticed the candles on the table with champagne, flowers, and fine China. "What's the occasion?"

"I love my wife," he expressed.

"She's a lucky woman," she concurred. "Well, I better be on my way. I don't want to spoil it for you." She walked to him, planted a kiss on his cheek and whispered, "Enjoy." Then as she was turning, she pulled his towel, exposing his nude body, just as Vinny entered.

"Well, did I interrupt anything?" she snarled.

Grabbing his towel, Chaz started, "Vinny, I…"

"Never mind!" she snapped then turned and ran out in tears.

"Vinny!" he yelled, but she was gone. "Damn it, Diamond! You play too much!"

"I'm sorry, Chaz. I'll talk to her."

"You've done quite enough, *thank you*!" he sarcastically snapped, then turned to run upstairs to put on clothes.

****

Vinny was so upset; she just drove with tears flowing down her face. She ignored several calls from her husband on her cell phone. Then suddenly, she realized she didn't know where she was. She was on her way to Shelby's house, and she knew that Shelby lived in the middle of nowhere, but this area didn't look familiar at all. She thought she knew every inch of this town, so she grew curious as to where she was. She stopped, dried her face with the handkerchief her grandmother had given to her years ago, and jumped out of her silver BMW. People were walking past her, but she didn't recognize anyone.

Vinny's handkerchief flew out of her hands, and she chased after it. When she finally retrieved it, she was in an alley. She looked up just as a person with a snake pinky ring shot another person. When the small group of people noticed her, she recognized some of them, including her brother, Frankie. It seemed like hours that she was plastered in that spot in a daze as the young man's bloody body crashed to the ground. "Vinny!" Frankie squeezed out.

"Get her!" She heard someone yell, and she took off running, dropping both her cell phone and the handkerchief.

Vinny's hands were shaking uncontrollably when she jumped into her car. She started up and drove off, searching for her cell phone, as she witnessed the people in her rear-view mirror running after her car. As she entered the main road, she remembered where Shelby's house was, and she sped into Shelby's driveway. Vinny banged on the door until Shelby's husband opened it. "Hi, Vinny," he greeted while Vinny entered the house with a folder in her hands.

"Hi, Tony. Where…?" She stopped when she saw Shelby enter the room.

"Hi, Valencia," she spoke, smiling wide. "What's up?"

Blowing hard, Vinny started, "I just saw…" She stopped suddenly, remembering that her brother was involved in a murder. Then she reasoned to herself that maybe that boy didn't die. Maybe he was just wounded. She concluded that she had better keep this to herself until she could find out more from Frankie. Vinny shook her head and stated, "Shelby, I need to talk to you."

"What is it, honey?"

Vinny handed her the folder and snapped, "You're stealing from me!"

"What?"

"Don't try to deny it. I checked it thoroughly. You have stolen over two hundred and fifty thousand dollars from me!"

"Two hun…?!" Tony started but his breath ran out. He couldn't believe his ears. If Shelby was stealing that kind of money from Vinny, where was it going?"

"Valencia, this can't be right!" Shelby squeezed out, looking at the paperwork.

"How could you do this to me?" Vinny went on. "I trusted you."

"Valencia, this isn't right! I swear!" she defended.

"It *is* right! I *checked* the receipts and *double*-checked with the bank! The inventory does not add up with the receipts, Shelby!" Vinny insisted, and Shelby just dropped in a chair with her head down. "I pay you a commission higher than any other artist pay their managers!" Shelby remained silent, and that infuriated Vinny even more, so she took a breath. "You're *fired*!" Shelby jerked up to look at her. But what Vinny blasted next caught Shelby totally by surprise. "I'm pressing charges, and you're going to *jail*!" Vinny turned and stormed out.

"Shelby, is this true?" Tony asked his wife, and she nodded slowly. "Why?"

"I did it for *her*," she defended. "I made her the biggest artist in the state, and that doesn't come cheap."

"Then why didn't you tell her?"

"Because I knew she wouldn't agree with my methods." Suddenly, Shelby jumped up and exclaimed, "I've got to stop her and explain it to her!"

****

As Vinny drove down the deserted, country road, she realized she must have dropped her cell phone in that alley. She was devastated. She didn't know what to do next. Her husband was cheating on her with her best friend. Her manager was robbing her blind. Her brother was involved in a murder. What else could happen! Suddenly, a car rushed to the side of her. She recognized it to be Shelby's black Cadillac Escalade. "Valencia, pull over!" Shelby called through the opened window. "I can explain."

Vinny rolled down her window and shouted, "Leave me alone, Shelby! I'm through with you!"

"Please, Valencia!" she yelled. "Hear me out!"

"I have *nothing* to say to you. You have betrayed me! Now leave...." Vinny started, but before she could finish, Shelby's car bumped into her car by accident, Vinny lost control of her car, and she went tumbling over the embankment, with both Shelby and her screaming wildly.

Shelby pulled her car over to the side, jumped out, and looked down the embankment. "Oh my God!" She took out her cell phone and started to call 911 but realized she had no service. "Oh, my God!" she blurted aloud. She knew it was probably too late for Vinny anyway. Vinny was probably dead already. She jumped back into her car and started driving in the opposite direction from her home.

When Shelby was further down the road, she blocked her number then dialed 911 to report the accident and hung up quickly. Then she wiped her tears and dialed another number. Mayor Carson answered, and she said, "Honey, meet me at the beach house."

"Now?"

"Yes, *now!*"

****

Chaz sat on the couch, calling everybody Vinny and he knew, to see if they knew where Vinny was. He was getting worried. She wasn't answering her cell phone. He had to explain to her that what she *thought* she saw wasn't true. He would *never* cheat on her. "Where are you, Vinny?" he pondered aloud, just as the doorbell rang. He rushed to the door, opened it quickly and was shocked to see two policemen standing there. "Mr. Perkins?" one policeman asked.

"Yes," he answered quickly. "What is it?"

"Your wife was in an accident."

"What kind of accident?"

"Car accident."

Taking a deep breath, Chaz inquired cautiously, "Is she all right?"

****

Mayor Jackson Carson opened the door of the beach house, and Shelby stormed in immediately. "What's wrong?" he asked.

"Valencia found out that I was skimming from the profits. The money I used to buy *this* house. The money *you* were *supposed* to pay back for me!"

"What did she say?"

"She said she's pressing charges."

"We'll talk to her together to straighten her out before she takes it that far, honey," he promised.

"Jackson, there's something else."

"What?"

She blew hard and explained, "I jumped into my car to try to stop her. I drove a little too close and accidentally bumped into her car. She lost control and her car went skidding over the embankment."

"What?!" he exploded. "Is she dead?"

"I don't know, but it was an *accident*!"

Pulling her in his arms, he comforted, "Honey, I believe you. I know you wouldn't hurt Vinny on purpose. You love that girl."

Looking deep into his eyes, she whimpered, "Baby, what am I going to do? I think she's *dead*!"

"It'll be all right, honey. Let's just cross one bridge at a time," he suggested then pulled her into his arms.

Part Six
Back to the Present

Chapter 20

"Honey, are you all right?" Chaz was asking Vinny, still supporting her limp body, drawing the attention of all the guests.

Nodding, Vinny squeezed out softly, "It was *you*!" Everyone witnessed that she was pointing at the mayor and his two aids. "It was *you* in the alley."

"What?" Mayor Carson chuckled.

"I can remember now," Vinny went on. "I remember your ring." She pointed to Elijah James with the snake pinky ring. "You killed Kenneth Lewis, but all of you were in that alley." As Chaz look back to focus on Detective Harper and the other two policemen, Mayor Carson grabbed Vinny and put a pocketknife to her neck while the women gasped.

"Everyone, just stay where you are," he demanded. "Elijah, get the car!" The mayor's aid rushed out.

"Jackson, what're you doing?" Tammie Carson asked, not believing what was happening.

"I've got to get out of the country!" he snapped.

Shelby stepped forward and inquired, "Jackson, what's going on?"

"I'm sorry, Shelby, but I have to leave," he shared as tears began rolling down her face. "I love you. That was *never* a lie." His wife focused on Shelby, realizing that *she* was his mistress.

"Mayor, it's all over," Chaz spoke up, taking Patrice's hand, to calm her. "Please let my wife go."

"Sorry, I can't do that. I can be out of the country in a few hours," he hypothesized. "If anyone tries to stop me, I'll gut her like a fish."

"No!" Patrice screamed, while Chaz supported her weight. "Jackson, please!"

Liam pulled out a 9mm Pistol and moved to the mayor for support, and the mayor's wife just stood frozen in the crowd, dumbfounded at everything that was unfolding before her eyes. Detective Harper and the other police officers unbuckled their gun belts, but they knew they couldn't make a move or Vinny would be dead.

"I'm sorry, Patrice." Mayor Carson replied, as he backed up with the knife still at Vinny's throat, pulling her with him.

"Please don't hurt her," Patrice begged.

"I won't hurt her if nobody interferes."

"Jackson, look at her," Patrice begged.

"What?"

"Look at Vinny," her mother demanded.

"Why would I want to do that?"

"Because she has *your* eyes," Patrice answered. "Jackson, she's *your* daughter."

"What?" he spat a little dazed.

"Please don't hurt *our* daughter," she pleaded, as they heard Elijah blowing the horn.

The mayor finally added, "Why didn't you tell me?"

"I didn't want to ruin your marriage and your career," she explained. "Look at her."

Just as Mayor Carson and Liam approached the doorway with Vinny, Frankie grabbed Liam, and his father chopped the mayor's hand, as Vinny dropped down, and Chaz grabbed her. Elijah was out of the car with a Glock while Liam broke free from Frankie, and Detective Harper, with the other two policemen opened fire with Elijah and Liam, while the women screamed.

Part Seven
One Month Later

Chapter 21

"Here you go, baby," Chaz offered, handing Vinny a glass of iced tea, then sat on the couch beside her to watch television, wearing blue pajama bottoms with Vinny wearing the top to them.

"Thank you," she accepted, smiling big. "I missed this."

"What...*tea*?" he joked.

"No, not *tea*!" she chuckled then sobered quickly. "I missed remembering all the Saturday mornings that we sat and just did *nothing* but *enjoy* each other."

They met in a sweet kiss. "I missed it too, sweetie."

"I am so sorry I jumped to the wrong conclusions about you and Diamond. I don't know what I was thinking. I know what a flirt Diamond is," she explained. "I guess I wasn't thinking straight because I was so upset about what Shelby had done."

"I'm glad you remembered the table was set for our anniversary," he added. "I cooked a wonderful dinner for you that evening...with your *mother's* help." They laughed together then met in another sweet kiss. "What have you decided to do about Shelby?"

She took a breath. "I decided not to press charges. Jackson Carson had her nose so wide open; she would've done *anything* for that man. She's going to pay me back by selling the beach house, their little love nest that she used the money for."

"That's nice of you."

"Well, she's been good to me," she shared, taking a sip of her tea.

"Do you have anyone else in mind to replace her?"

She shook her head. "No. Not yet. Shelby will be hard to replace."

"Are you thinking about keeping her?"

"I don't know if I can trust her again," she explained. "This job is probably all she has to look forward to now-a-days. I probably will keep her but with restrictions."

"Just think hard and pray about it before you make any decisions," he suggested, and she nodded. "How is Shelby doing with the death of Jackson Carson?"

"She's taking it rather hard. She really loved him."

"He said he loved her too," he acknowledged.

"Yes, he did."

"What about her husband. Is he staying with her?"

"No. They're getting a divorce. She doesn't love him," she explained. "She's really broken up about good ole dad, but she's strong. She'll make it through. It's just going to take time."

Mayor Jackson Carson and his two aids were killed in the shootout. Frankie was shot in the leg and had to go back into the hospital. Frankie shared with the authorities that they had a gun trafficking ring going on for years. Kenneth Lewis became addicted to drugs and started stealing the money. He said that if they hadn't gotten rid of Kenneth, the arms dealers they were doing business with would have gotten rid of *them*. Frankie's trial will come up soon. His lawyer thinks he will get a light sentence because he is cooperating and naming some very important people who were involved. Authorities have already made some arrests.

"I've got to start interviewing people for Brooke's position since she accepted that principal's job at the middle school."

"Good for her."

"Yes, she deserves it. She works hard, and it takes some pressure off me. She and Monica were *really* not getting alone."

"I wondered when that relationship was going to turn toxic."

"Well, it did," he confirmed. "What about Lance Greene? Are you going back to see him?"

"I don't think so. He knows he isn't my father, and he really has never been a dad to me anyway," she explained, as the doorbell rang. "I wonder who that could be." He rose and helped her up, and they walked to the door together.

"Ma!" Vinny exploded at the door, standing right behind her husband.

"I hope I'm not interrupting anything. I just came right over after work," Patrice explained, standing there in her work uniform.

"No problem." he responded. "Please come in."

"How are you, Ma?" Vinny inquired, sitting beside her mother on the couch.

"I'm okay."

"Mama Pat, would you like some iced tea?" Chaz offered.

"No, thank you, son."

"Okay, I'll give you two some privacy," he suggested then left.

"Ma, what's wrong?"

"Vinny," she pondered then took a deep breath. "I need to talk to you about what you learned at your show. It took me this long to build up enough nerves to come and see you."

"It doesn't matter, Ma."

"It matters to me," she insisted then took another deep breath. "Honey, I'm sorry I never told you who your real father was."

"It's okay. Really."

"No, it isn't okay. All children have a right to know who their parents are. It was wrong of me to deny you that right," her mother explained. "I hope you will forgive me one day."

"Mom, there's nothing to forgive. You gave me a great dad when you married Milo."

"I'm glad you and Milo get along so well. You deserved a good father in your life since I denied you of your real one."

"Although you had me very young, you were a great mother to me. You never put your needs above mine. I love you. Nothing will *ever* change that," Vinny explained, taking her mother's hand.

"Thank you, sweetheart," her mother replied with a few tears running down her face, and Vinny handed her some Kleenex from the coffee table. Patrice dabbed her tears then blew hard. "Vinny, I was a rebellious teenager. My mother was super religious, and I was sick and tired of her throwing God up in my face." She paused. "I was young and dumb. I didn't know any better. I'm not using it as an excuse, but I just want you to understand." Vinny nodded with a sweet smile. "I started working at the restaurant when I was fifteen because I wanted my own money." She paused briefly before continuing. "One day at work, this *gorgeous* man came in. He was the most handsome man I had ever seen in my life. And when he smiled at me, I was in love. I knew the family, but I had never met him because he was quite a bit older than I was. But I asked around, and I learned that his name was Jackson Carson, and he had just finished law school and had signed up with this big law firm in another town, which he and his pregnant wife moved to. But since his mother still lived here, he would visit often." She paused. "He moved his mother out of the housing projects and bought a house for her and his siblings. I had so much respect for him." Vinny touched her hand lovingly. Her mother continued, "One day I was walking home from work, and he stopped and asked if I wanted a ride. I was so flattered, I jumped in right away. He asked me if I wanted to go to the beach, and I couldn't say yes quick enough." She paused. "He rented us a room, and we made love."

"So, it wasn't rape?"

"Oh no, honey. I was so much in love with that man, I would've done *anything* for him," she explained. "He was so gentle and refreshing from anybody I had ever known. I felt like a princess, being in a beautiful hotel room, and not behind the school bleachers or in the backseat of a car." She paused again to blow her nose. "Whenever he would come to town, we would get together. Then one day he ended it. His wife had a miscarriage, and he said he felt guilty and could not do this to her anymore. Although I was devastated, I understood. To drown my sorrows, I started seeing Lance. He would always flirt with me in the restaurant, so after about a week, I invited him to my house. I knew my mother was at a church revival and would be gone most of the night." She paused again. "We made love. It was sweet, but not as sweet as with Jackson because I didn't love him. Suddenly, the door flew open, and my angry mother was standing there. She called the police and had Lance arrested immediately. When I found out I was pregnant, everyone just assumed it was Lance's, and since he was in jail, I didn't correct them. I intended to tell Jackson about the baby, but the next time I saw him, he was with his wife and had plans to move back here and run for a city councilman's seat, and I didn't want to destroy him."

"I understand, Ma," Vinny finally replied, wiping her own tears. Then she pulled her weeping mother in her arms and hugged her lovingly. "I understand."

****

Parker was in the shower when he heard the shower door open. He opened his eyes and Sabrina was smiling big, stepping in there with him. "Baby, you're home!" he exploded.

Moving in his arms, she cooed, "Are you happy?" He just smiled and kissed her lovingly.

"I missed you."

"I missed you too," she shared. "I hear the show ended with a bang *literally*, but was it a huge success?"

"Baby, we sold *everything* and have orders for *future* paintings," he shared, smiling wide.

"Awesome!"

"When is your next tour?"

"Not until next year."

"That's the best news I've heard all morning," he remarked, kissing her again. Then out of the blue, he asked, "Sabrina, will you marry me?" Her mouth dropped open as she vigorously nodded her head, too choked to speak. Then he grabbed her and kissed her lovingly. "I know that wasn't the most romantic way to do this, but I just couldn't wait. I love you."

"I love you, too," she shared, and their lips met again in a long, passionate kiss as the warm water massaged their bodies.

Parker wanted to tell Sabrina about what happened between Justine and him, but he knew Sabrina wouldn't handle it very well, and he really didn't want to lose her. What happened between Justine and him was a one-time thing, and he didn't want to lose Sabrina over a one-time mistake. He didn't even know *why* it happened. He supposed he was just lonesome when Sabrina was away. He knew that wasn't an excuse, but that's all he could think of because he really and truly loved her. He thought, *I guess all marriages have a few secrets. If every couple knew everything about each other, there would be no marriages taking place at all.* Sabrina was wrapping her legs around his waist, and his body was reacting immediately. He knew then that he would spend the rest of his life making it up to her, and she would have no idea why he was so *good* to her.

****

"Honey, are you all right?" Chaz called, walking up the stairs. After her mother left, Vinny had gone to take a shower, and he hadn't seen her return to the den, so he grew concerned. "Honey!"

When he opened the bedroom door, she was lying on the bed stark naked. His body quivered with excitement. "I remember something else," she confessed, while he stood there staring at her lovely, pecan-tanned body.

"What's that. Mrs. Perkins?"

"I remember our Saturday morning rendezvous." She winked at him. "Has that changed?" He couldn't get his clothes off fast enough as she chuckled at his enthusiasm.

She loved her husband so much, and he loved her. She was sorry for the few months she couldn't remember their life together. He was a wonderful man, and she was blessed to have him. She exhaled deeply, feeling the warmth of her husband's love. She was thankful to have her memory back since some memories are worth remembering and keeping in your heart *forever*.

The End

Thank you for reading my book.

Please read my other books:

Consequences: a novel of friendship that is centered around three lifelong friends: Cecily, a pediatrician who became involved with organized crime when she paid her way through medical school as a call-girl, which becomes a living nightmare for her; Lillian, a housewife turned alcoholic, who fights hard and steady for her husband, who has a philandering desire for Cecily; and Trudy, a wild and spirited fashion model, who finds comfort in the arms of Cecily's ex-pimp, turning to food at her heartbreak, achieving obesity and a failing career. Please get your copy today.

Sister Lucy: depicts church leaders in their fallible lives, their chaotic entanglements, and their struggles with temptations. The novel opens with a mystery that would lead to a "spiritual conclusion." Not everything is peachy with the ministers and preachers of the St. John Fellowship Community Church. Beyond the sermons and the hymns, they are stuck in illicit affairs, spiritual crises, and lies. Sister Lucy Davis, one of the ministers, sings like an angel but her heart cries out with guilt and discontent, as she struggles to reassess her faith and to find her way out of dead-end relationships. Unknown to Lucy, her misadventures are pushing her into danger. At one point, Lucy scans the mess in her life, wondering what the heck happened to that church-going woman who was always ready to extend a helping hand. Lucy Davis' latest boyfriend is none other than Reverend Clyde Mitchell, a charismatic leader who finds pleasure in the beds of all women except his wife's. Rev. Mitchell's son Kip, a handsome detective, struggles to be faithful to the ideals of his religion but covets Lucy. Minister Samantha Marsh further complicates matters by plotting to ensnare Kip.

Sister Lucy II (Kip & Lucy): a continuous novel about the struggles, triumphs, victories, obstacles, and faith of the saved and the not so saved. It is centered around the handsome and charming Pastor Kip Mitchell and his lovely wife Lucy, as they continue their lives together in love and happiness, with trouble lurking behind every nook and cranny. Kip and Lucy quickly find out that the devil doesn't have new tricks, just new people. Dr. Robin Bonner has set her sights on Kip. She sets her traps carefully for him as she tries desperately to hide from a tormenting past, while etching a place in the heart of Dr. Julius Hammond. Just as Dr. Bonner feels that she is making progress with snaring Kip, a long-time buried truth is revealed that could change all their lives.

Single Mom: Carla David was a mother of three, living a dream life with Brandon, the man of her dreams. Until one day, without either forewarning or expectation, he tells her that he doesn't want to be married anymore. To say Carla was either shocked or bewildered would be a drastic understatement, because she had neither education nor gainful employment and is in dire fear of what to do next. Carla soon learns that Brandon had been harboring a secret, which jolts her into reality that she is a single mom, and she does not have time to wallow in pity, but pick herself up, step up to the plate, and take care of her children. What Carla does will not only inspire single moms everywhere, but it will encourage them as well, as they witness her transformation growing from a weak, self-pity married woman to a strong, vibrant single mom who will put herself in harm's way to protect her children at any cost. *Single Mom* is a story of survival for all who have felt that their lives were over, because of a situation that was not under their control. *Single Mom* will inspire readers through a spiritual, emotional, and triumphant journey, with a heart wrenching story of commitment, survival, danger, betrayal, and love as seen through the eyes of a single mom.

Toni Talk: a journey of the lives of Toni Melton, an acclaimed, nationally recognized ambitious outspoken journalist of the famous column, *Toni Talk*; and her illustrious husband, Ron Joyner, a criminal defense attorney who has ambitions of his own. While Toni strives to become a Pulitzer Prize winner and Ron pushes to become a partner in his law firm, they bump heads in the worst way. Toni and Ron encounter some devious foes along the way who would like nothing better than to tear their perfect little love nest down. Just when Toni and Ron are at the top of their professions, ready to break loose with insurmountable feats, a detrimental article appears in *Toni Talk*, causing Ron to become faced with a multi-million-dollar lawsuit, disbarment, and unemployment.

Soon to be released:
Second Chance: a heart-warming story of love and envy, set in a well-rounded trilogy of strife, religion, heartache, and closure. *Second Chance* evolves around the entanglement of Marcus, a charismatic, intelligent, easy-spirited lawyer, who is torn between his past love, Karen, a high-strung, television News Anchorwoman, who left him at the altar fifteen years ago; and his present love, Saundra, a Christian, OB/GYN Doctor, who is now his fiancée and Karen's long-time rival. *Second Chance* has captured the hearts and minds of people experiencing heartache, misery, and strife. Read it with a box of tissues because this story will tantalize your heart and tug at your emotions with every tear-filled page of drive, commitment, and desire. *Second Chance* awakens love, motives, morals, drives, and attitudes of the entanglement of people in their fallible lives

to arrive at a burning conclusion, to achieve a lasting impression, exploring the all-powerful question: *Do you deserve a second chance?*

About the Author:

Dr. Lurma Swinney is a native of South Carolina. Her passion is writing. She is a Christian and credits God for everything good in her life. Dr. Swinney started writing at a young age but did not become serious about writing until she became an adult. Dr. Swinney has worked in schools throughout South Carolina and New Jersey. She earned her Ph.D. from Capella University in Minneapolis, Minnesota. Dr. Swinney is a member of Alpha Kappa Alpha Sorority Incorporated. She writes to inspire, educate, and encourage all people. This book marks Dr. Swinney's sixth published novel. Please visit her website at sdpublishinghouse.com. You may also email her at swinney@sdpublishinghouse.com. She would love to hear from you.

Thank you for your support!

Forgotten Memories

Lurma Swinney, PhD

www.ingramcontent.com/pod-product-compliance
Lightning Source LLC
LaVergne TN
LVHW031604060526
838200LV00055B/4481